The Rupa Book of Scary Stories

Ruskin Bond has been writing for over sixty years, and has now over 120 titles in print—novels, collections of stories, poetry, essays, anthologies and books for children. His first novel, *The Room on the Roof*, received the prestigious John Llewellyn Rhys Prize in 1957.

He has also received the Padma Shri (1999), the Padma Bhushan (2014) and two awards from the Sahitya Akademi—one for his short stories and another for his writings for children. In 2012, the Delhi government gave him its Lifetime Achievement Award. Born in 1934, Ruskin Bond grew up in Jamnagar, Shimla, New Delhi and Dehradun. Apart from three years in the UK, he has spent all his life in India, and now lives in Mussoorie with his adopted family.

The Rupa Book of Scary Stories

REVISED AND UPDATED EDITION

Edited by
Ruskin Bond

RUPA

First published in 2013 in 2013
Rupa Publications India Pvt. Ltd
7/16, Ansari Road, Daryaganj
New Delhi 110002

Sales Centres:

Allahabad Bengaluru Chennai
Hyderabad Jaipur Kathmandu
Kolkata Mumbai

ISBN: 978-81-291-0389-5

Sixth impression 2019

10 9 8 7 6

Typeset in Nikita Overseas Pvt Ltd. New Delhi

Contents

Introduction

If there's one thing I've learnt in the course of a long writing life, it's that young readers love getting a scare. I do, too, provided it's only on the printed page.

Offer a fourteen-year old a choice between reading a book of love stories or a collection of ghost stories, and nine times out of ten the ghost stories will win hands down. Lovers are inclined to be predictable. Ghosts, never!

Occasionally, a reader comes up to me with the complaint: 'Sir, your ghosts aren't frightening enough. They're so friendly!' Young readers don't want friendly ghosts, they want scary ghosts—or werewolves, vampires, witches, maniacs, and monsters of all kinds! And so, to compensate for all the harmless ghosts I've created or presented over the years, I have chosen a set of stories guaranteed to make the reader (regardless of his or her age) shiver, shudder, and look under the bed before sleeping with the lights on.

Not all the stories in this collection are about the supernatural. There are no ghosts in 'Henry' or 'Boomerang' but they are among the most frightening stories I have ever read. Terror comes from the unexpected, the uninvited, the unexplained. The stories by Saki and WW Jacobs carry the horrific little twist that we have come to associate with these writers.

Nevertheless, the supernatural element is a strong one. Algernon Blackwood was a master of the genre, and 'The Empty House' is a classic on the theme of...well, empty houses and whatever lurks within them.

Rudyard Kipling wrote a number of successful ghost stories, most of them set in India. I first heard the story of 'The Phantom Rickshaw' from my father, who took me up to Simla in 1943, to admit me to a boarding-school. During the mid-term break he took me for a rickshaw ride around Elysium hill, and on the way he recounted Kipling's story. It was the last time I saw him. And it wasn't until many years later that I read the original. One of Kipling's best. And his eerie little tale, 'At the Pit's Mouth', though not really a ghost story, sent a shiver down my spine. As did another Simla apparition in my own brief contribution, 'A Face in the Night'.

Three stories set in Simla! Have I deserted Mussoorie, you might well ask. Not so. It's just a supernatural coincidence.

The East End of London, which I explored as a young man, provided the background for Thomas Burke's powerful stories. One of his best, 'The Hollow Man', is presented here. Arthur Morrison was another fine writer who went to the poorer parts of London and Paris for his haunting tales. Oscar Cook spent many years in North Borneo, and a number of his chilling tales are set in that mysterious region.

Let me just add that most of the stories in this collection are great short stories in their own right. Beautifully crafted, stylish, and written with a fluency and clarity that is rare in modern writers. That they are scary or entertaining adds to their readability; but you can enjoy them as literature too. 'The Monkey's Paw' is one of the most moving stories I have ever read. And as a play it has been enthusiastically performed by generations of school students the world over.

Ruskin Bond
June 2003

The Empty House

BY ALGERNON BLACKWOOD

Certain houses, like certain persons, manage somehow to proclaim at once their character for evil. In the case of the latter, no particular feature need betray them; they may boast an open countenance and an ingenuous smile; and yet a little of their company leaves the unalterable conviction that there is something radically amiss with their being: that they are evil. Willy nilly, they seem to communicate an atmosphere of secret and wicked thoughts which makes those in their immediate neighbourhood shrink from them as from a thing diseased.

And, perhaps, with houses the same principle is operative, and it is the aroma of evil deeds committed under a particular roof, long after the actual doers have passed away, that makes the gooseflesh come and the hair rise. Something of the original passion of the evil-doer, and of the horror felt by his victim, enters the heart of the innocent watcher, and he becomes suddenly conscious of tingling nerves, creeping skin, and a chilling of the blood. He is terror-stricken without apparent cause.

There was manifestly nothing in the external appearance of this particular house to bear out the tales of the horror that was said to reign within. It was neither lonely nor unkempt. It stood, crowded into a corner of the square, and looked exactly like the houses on either side of it. It had the same number of windows as its neighbours; the same balcony overlooking the gardens; the same white steps leading up to the heavy black front door; and, in the rear, there was the same narrow strip of green, with neat box borders, running up to the wall that divided it from the backs of the adjoining houses. Apparently, too, the number of chimney pots on the roof was the same; the breadth and angle of the eaves; and even the height of the dirty area railings.

And yet this house in the square, that seemed precisely similar to its fifty ugly neighbours, was as a matter of fact entirely different—horribly different.

Wherein lay this marked, invisible difference is impossible to say. It cannot be ascribed wholly to the imagination, because persons who had spent some time in the house, knowing nothing of the facts, had declared positively that certain rooms were so disagreeable they would rather die than enter them again, and that the atmosphere of the whole house produced in them symptoms of a genuine terror; while the series of innocent tenants who had tried to live in it and been forced to decamp at the shortest possible notice, was indeed little less than a scandal in the town.

When Shorthouse arrived to pay a 'weekend' visit to his Aunt Julia in her little house on the seafront at the other end of the town, he found her charged to the brim with mystery and excitement. He had only received her telegram that morning, and he had come anticipating boredom; but the moment he touched her hand and kissed her apple-skin wrinkled cheek, he caught the first waves of her electrical condition. The impression deepened when he learned that there were to be no other visitors, and that he had been telegraphed for with a very special object.

Something was in the wind, and the 'something' would doubtless bear fruit; for this elderly spinster aunt, with a mania for psychical research, had brains as well as willpower, and by hook or by crook she usually managed to accomplish her ends. The revelation was made soon after tea, when she sidled close up to him as they paced slowly along the seafront in the dusk.

'I've got the keys,' she announced in a delighted, yet half awesome voice. 'Got them till Monday!'

'The keys of the bathing-machine, or—?' he asked innocently, looking from the sea to the town. Nothing brought her so quickly to the point as feigning stupidity.

'Neither,' she whispered. 'I've got the keys of the haunted house in the square—and I'm going there tonight.'

Shorthouse was conscious of the slightest possible tremor down his back. He dropped his teasing tone. Something in her voice and manner thrilled him. She was in earnest.

'But you can't go alone—' he began.

'That's why I wired for you,' she said with decision.

He turned to look at her. The ugly, lined, enigmatical face was alive with excitement. There was the glow of genuine enthusiasm round it like a halo. The eyes shone. He caught another wave of her excitement, and a second tremor, more marked than the first, accompanied it.

'Thanks, Aunt Julia,' he said politely; 'thanks awfully.'

'I should not dare to go quite alone,' she went on, raising her voice; 'But with you I should enjoy it immensely. You're afraid of nothing, I know.'

'Thanks *so* much,' he said again. 'Er—is anything likely to happen?'

'A great deal *has* happened,' she whispered, 'though it's been most cleverly hushed up. Three tenants have come and gone in the last few months, and the house is said to be empty for good now.'

In spite of himself Shorthouse became interested. His aunt was so very much in earnest.

'The house is very old indeed,' she went on, 'and the story—an unpleasant one—dates a long way back. It has to do with a murder committed by a jealous stableman who had some affair with a servant in the house. One night he managed to secrete himself in the cellar, and when everyone was asleep, he crept upstairs to the servants' quarters, chased the girl down to the next landing, and before anyone could come to the rescue threw her bodily over the banisters into the hall below.'

'And the stableman——?'

'Was caught, I believe, and hanged for murder; but it all happened a century ago, and I've not been able to get more details of the story.'

Shorthouse now felt his interest thoroughly aroused but, though he was not particularly nervous for himself, he hesitated a little on his aunt's account.

'On one condition,' he said at length.

'Nothing will prevent my going,' she said firmly; 'but I may as well hear your condition.'

'That you guarantee your power of self-control if anything really horrible happens. I mean—that you are sure you won't get too frightened.'

'Jim,' she said scornfully 'I'm not young, I know, nor are my nerves; but *with you* I should be afraid of nothing in the world!'

This, of course, settled it, for Shorthouse had no pretensions to being other than a very ordinary young man, and an appeal to his vanity was irresistible. He agreed to go.

Instinctively, by a sort of sub-conscious preparation, he kept himself and his forces well in hand the whole evening, compelling an accumulative reserve of control by that nameless inward process of gradually putting all the emotions away and turning the key upon them—a process difficult to describe, but wonderfully effective, as all men who have lived through severe trials of the inner man well understand. Later, it stood him in good stead.

But it was not until half-past ten, when they stood in the hall, well in the glare of friendly lamps and still surrounded by comforting human influences, that he had to make the first call upon this store of collected strength. For, once the door was closed, and he saw the deserted silent street stretching away white in the moonlight before them, it came to him clearly that the real test that night would be in dealing with *two fears* instead of one. He would have to carry his aunt's fear as well as his own. And, as he glanced down at her sphinx-like countenance and realized that it might assume no pleasant aspect in a rush of real terror, he felt satisfied with only one thing in the whole adventure—that he had confidence in his own will and power to stand against any shock that might come.

Slowly they walked along the empty streets of the town; a bright autumn moon silvered the roofs, casting deep shadows; there was no breath of wind; and the trees in the formal gardens by the seafront watched them silently as they passed along. To his aunt's occasional remarks Shorthouse made no reply, realizing that she was simply surrounding herself with mental buffers—saying ordinary things to prevent herself thinking of extraordinary things. Few windows showed lights, and from scarcely a single chimney came smoke or sparks. Shorthouse had already begun to notice everything, even the smallest details. Presently they stopped at the street corner and looked up at the name on the side of the house full in the moonlight, and with one accord, but without remark, turned into the square and crossed over to the side of it that lay in shadow.

'The number of the house is thirteen,' whispered a voice at his side; and neither of them made the obvious reference, but passed across the broad sheet of moonlight and began to march up the pavement in silence.

It was about halfway up the square that Shorthouse felt an arm slipped quietly but significantly into his own, and knew then that their adventure had begun in earnest, and that his companion was already yielding imperceptibly to the influences against them. She needed support.

A few minutes later they stopped before a tall, narrow house that rose before them into the night, ugly in shape and painted a dingy white. Shutterless windows, without blinds, stared down upon them, shining here and there in the moonlight. There were weather streaks in the wall and cracks in the paint, and the balcony bulged out from the first floor a little unnaturally. But, beyond this generally forlorn appearance of an unoccupied house, there was nothing at first sight to single out this particular mansion for the evil character it had most certainly acquired.

Taking a look over their shoulders to make sure they had not been followed, they went boldly up the steps and stood against the huge black door that fronted them forbiddingly. But the first wave of nervousness was now upon them, and Shorthouse fumbled a long time with the key before he could fit it into the lock at all. For a moment, if truth were told, they both hoped it would not open, for they were a prey to various unpleasant emotions as they stood there on the threshold of their ghostly adventure. Shorthouse, shuffling with the key and hampered by the steady weight on his arm, certainly felt the solemnity of the moment. It was as if the whole world—for all experience seemed at that instant concentrated in his own consciousness—were listening to the grating noise of that key. A stray puff of wind wandering down the empty street woke a momentary rustling in the trees behind them, but otherwise this rattling of the key was the only sound audible; and at last it turned in the lock and the heavy door swung open and revealed a yawning gulf of darkness beyond.

With a last glance at the moonlit square, they passed quickly in, and the door slammed behind them with a roar that echoed prodigiously through empty halls and passages. But, instantly, with the echoes, another sound made itself heard, and Aunt Julia leaned suddenly so heavily upon him that he had to take a step backwards to save himself from falling.

A man had coughed close beside them—so close that it seemed they must have been actually by his side in the darkness.

With the possibility of practical jokes in his mind, Shorthouse at once swung his heavy stick in the direction of the sound; but it met nothing more solid than air. He heard his aunt give a little gasp beside him.

'There's someone here,' she whispered, 'I heard him.'

'Be quiet!' he said sternly. 'It was nothing but the noise of the front door.'

'Oh! Get a light—quick!' she added, as her nephew, fumbling with a box of matches, opened it upside down and let them all fall with a rattle on to the stone floor.

The sound, however, was not repeated; and there was no evidence of retreating footsteps. In another minute they had a candle burning, using an empty end of a cigar case as a holder; and when the first flare had died down he held the impromptu lamp aloft and surveyed the scene. And it was dreary enough in all conscience, for there is nothing more desolate in all the abodes of men than an unfurnished house dimly lit, silent, and forsaken, and yet tenanted by rumour with the memories of evil and violent histories.

They were standing in a wide hallway; on their left was the open door of a spacious dining room, and in front the hall ran, ever narrowing, into a long, dark passage that led apparently to the top of the kitchen stairs. The broad uncarpeted staircase rose in a sweep before them, everywhere draped in shadows, except for a single spot about halfway up where the moonlight came in through the window and fell on a bright patch on the boards. This shaft of light shed a faint radiance above and below it, lending to the objects within its reach a misty outline that was infinitely more suggestive and ghostly than complete darkness. Filtered moonlight always seems to paint faces on the surrounding gloom, and as Shorthouse peered up into the well of darkness and thought of the countless empty rooms and passages in the upper part of the old house, he caught himself longing again for the safety of the moonlit square, or the cosy, bright drawing room they had left an hour before. Then realizing that these thoughts were dangerous, he thrust them away again and summoned all his energy for concentration on the present.

'Aunt Julia,' he said aloud, severely, 'we must now go through the house from top to bottom and make a thorough search.'

The echoes of his voice died away slowly all over the building, and in the intense silence that followed he turned to look at her. In the candlelight he saw that her face was already ghastly pale; but she dropped his arm for a moment and said in a whisper, stepping close in front of him—

'I agree. We must be sure there's no one hiding. That's the first thing.'

She spoke with evident effort, and he looked at her with admiration.

'You feel quite sure of yourself? It's not too late——'

'I think so,' she whispered, her eyes shifting nervously toward the shadows behind. 'Quite sure, only one thing——'

'What's that?'

'You must never leave me alone for an instant.'

'As long as you understand that any sound or appearance must be investigated at once, for to hesitate means to admit fear. That is fatal.'

'Agreed,' she said, a little shakily, after a moment's hesitation. 'I'll try——'

Arm in arm, Shorthouse holding the dripping candle and the sack, while his aunt carried the cloak over her shoulders, figures of utter comedy to all but themselves, they began a systematic search.

Stealthily, walking on tip-toe and shading the candle lest it should betray their presence through the shutterless windows, they went first into the big dining room. There was not a stick of furniture to be seen. Bare walls, ugly mantel-pieces and empty grates stared at them. Everything, they felt, resented their intrusion, watching them, as it were, with veiled eyes; whispers followed them; shadows flitted noiselessly to right and left; something seemed ever at their back, watching, waiting an opportunity to do them injury. There was the inevitable sense that operations which went on when the room was empty had been temporarily suspended till they were well out of the way again. The whole dark interior of the old building seemed to become a malignant Presence that rose up, warning them to desist and mind their own business; every moment the strain on the nerves increased.

Out of the gloomy dining room they passed through large folding doors into a sort of library or smoking room, wrapt equally in silence, darkness, and dust; and from this they regained the hall near the top of the back stairs.

Here a pitch black tunnel opened before them into the lower regions, and—it must be confessed—they hesitated. But only for a minute. With the worst of the night still to come it was essential to turn from nothing. Aunt Julia stumbled at the top step of the dark descent, ill-lit by the flickering candle, and even. Shorthouse felt at least half the decision go out of his legs.

'Come on!' he said peremptorily, and his voice ran on and lost itself in the dark, empty spaces below.

'I'm coming,' she faltered, catching his arm with unnecessary violence.

They went a little unsteadily down the stone steps, a cold, damp air meeting them in the face, close and malodorous. The kitchen, into which the stairs led along a narrow passage, was large, with a lofty ceiling. Several doors opened out of it—some into cupboards with empty jars still standing on the shelves, and others into horrible little ghostly back offices, each colder and less inviting than the last. Black beetles scurried over the floor, and once, when they knocked against a deal table standing in a corner, something about the size of a cat jumped down with a rush and fled, scampering across the stone floor into the darkness. Everywhere there was a sense of recent occupation, an impression of sadness and gloom.

Leaving the main kitchen, they next went towards the scullery. The door was standing ajar, and as they pushed it open to its full extent Aunt Julia uttered a piercing scream, which she instantly tried to stifle by placing her hand over her mouth. For a second Shorthouse stood stock-still, catching his breath. He felt as if his spine had suddenly become hollow and someone had filled it with particles of ice.

Facing them, directly in their way between the doorposts, stood the figure of a woman. She had dishevelled hair and wildly staring eyes and her face was terrified and white as death.

She stood there motionless for the space of a single second. Then the candle flickered and she was gone—gone utterly—and the door framed nothing but empty darkness.

'Only the beastly jumping candle-light,' he said quickly, in a voice that sounded like someone else's and was only half under control. 'Come on, aunt. There's nothing there.'

He dragged her forward. With a clattering of feet and a great appearance of boldness they went on, but over his body the skin moved as if crawling ants covered it, and he knew by the weight on his arm that he was supplying the force of locomotion for two. The scullery was cold, bare, and empty; more like a large prison cell than anything else. They went round it, tried the door into the yard, and the windows, but found them all fastened securely. His aunt moved beside him like a person in a dream. Her eyes were tightly shut, and she seemed merely to follow the pressure of his arm. Her courage filled him with amazement. At the same time he noticed that a certain odd change had come over her face, a change which somehow evaded his power of analysis.

'There's nothing here, aunty,' he repeated aloud quickly, 'Let's go upstairs and see the rest of the house. Then we'll choose a room to wait up in.'

She followed him obediently, keeping close to his side, and they locked the kitchen door behind them. It was a relief to get up again. In the hall there was more light than before, for the moon had travelled a little further down the stairs. Cautiously they began to go up into the dark vault of the upper house, the boards creaking under their weight.

On the first floor they found the large double drawing rooms, a search of which revealed nothing. Here also was no sign of furniture or recent occupancy; nothing but dust and neglect and shadows. They opened the big folding doors between front and back drawing rooms and then came out again to the landing and went on upstairs.

They had not gone up more than a dozen steps when they both simultaneously stopped to listen, looking into each other's eyes with a new apprehension across the flickering candle flame. From the room they had left hardly ten seconds before came the sound of doors quietly closing. It was beyond all question; they heard the booming noise that accompanies the shutting of heavy doors, followed by the sharp catching of the latch.

'We must go back and see,' said Shorthouse briefly, in a low tone, and turning to go downstairs again.

Somehow she managed to drag after him, her feet catching in her dress, her face livid.

When they entered the front drawing room it was plain that the folding doors had been closed—half a minute before. Without hesitation Shorthouse opened them. He almost expected to see someone facing him in the back room; but only darkness and cold air met him. They went through both rooms, finding nothing unusual. They tried in every way to make the doors close of themselves, but there was not wind enough even to set the candle flame flickering. The doors would not move without strong pressure. All was silent as the grave. Undeniably the rooms were utterly empty, and the house utterly still.

'It's beginning,' whispered a voice at his elbow which he hardly recognized as his aunt's.

He nodded acquiescence, taking out his watch to note the time. It was fifteen minutes before midnight; he made the entry of exactly what had occurred in his notebook, setting the candle in its case upon the floor in order to do so. It took a moment or two to balance it safely against the wall.

Aunt Julia always declared that at this moment she was not actually watching him, but had turned her head towards the inner room, where she fancied she heard something moving; but, at any rate, both positively agreed that there came a sound of rushing feet, heavy and very swift—and the next instant the candle was out!

But to Shorthouse himself had come more than this, and he has always thanked his fortunate stars that it came to him alone and not to his aunt too. For, as he rose from the stooping position of balancing the candle, and before it was actually extinguished, a face thrust itself forward so close to his own that he could almost have touched it with his lips. It was a face working with passion; a man's face, dark, with thick features, and angry, savage eyes. It belonged to a common man, and it was evil in its ordinary normal expression, no doubt, but as he saw it, alive with intense, aggressive emotion it was a malignant and terrible human countenance.

There was no movement of the air: nothing but the sound of rushing feet—stockinged or muffed feet; the apparition of the face; and the almost simultaneous extinguishing of the candle.

In spite of himself, Shorthouse uttered a little cry, nearly losing his balance as his aunt clung to him with her whole weight in one moment of real, uncontrollable terror. She made no sound, but simply seized him bodily. Fortunately, however, she had seen nothing, but had only heard the rushing feet, for her control returned almost at once, and he was able to disentangle himself and strike a match.

The shadows ran away on all sides before the glare, and his aunt stooped down and groped for the cigar case with the precious candle. Then they discovered that the candle had not been *blown* out at all; it had been *crushed* out. The wick was pressed down into the wax, which was flattened as if by some smooth, heavy instrument.

How his companion so quickly overcame her terror, Shorthouse never properly understood; but his admiration for her self-control increased tenfold, and at the same time served to feed his own dying flame—for which he was undeniably grateful. Equally inexplicable to him was the evidence of physical force they had just witnessed. He at once suppressed the memory of stories he had heard of 'physical mediums' and their dangerous phenomena; for if these were true, and either his aunt or himself was unwittingly a physical medium, it meant that they were simply aiding to focus the forces of a haunted house already charged to the brim. It was like walking with unprotected lamps among uncovered stores of gunpowder.

So, with as little reflection as possible, he simply re-lit the candle and went up to the next floor. The arm in his trembled, it is true, and his own tread was often uncertain, but they went on with thoroughness, and after a search revealing nothing they climbed the last flight of stairs to the top floor of all.

Here they found a perfect nest of small servants' rooms, with broken pieces of furniture, dirty cane-bottomed chairs, chests of drawers, cracked mirrors, and decrepit bedsteads. The rooms had low sloping ceilings already hung here and there with cobwebs, small windows, and badly plastered walls—a depressing and dismal region which they were glad to leave behind.

It was on the stroke of midnight when they entered a small room on the third floor, close to the top of the stairs, and arranged to make themselves comfortable for the remainder of their adventure. It was absolutely bare, and was said to be the room—then used as a clothes closet—into which the infuriated groom had chased his victim and finally caught her. Outside, across the narrow landing, began the stairs leading up to the floor above, and the servants' quarters where they had just searched.

In spite of the chilliness of the night there was something in the air of this room that cried for an open window. But there was more than this. Shorthouse could only describe it by saying that he felt less master of himself here than in any other part of the house. There was something that acted directly on the nerves, tiring the resolution, enfeebling the will. He was conscious of this result before he had been in the room five minutes, and it was in the short time they stayed there that he suffered the wholesale depletion of his vital forces, which was, for himself, the chief horror of the whole experience.

They put the candle on the floor of the cupboard, leaving the door a few inches ajar, so that there was no glare to confuse the eyes, and no shadow to shift about on walls and ceiling. Then they spread the cloak on the floor and sat down to wait, with their backs against the wall.

Shorthouse was within two feet of the door on to the landing; his position commanded a good view of the main staircase leading down into the darkness, and also of the beginning of the servants' stairs going to the floor above; the heavy stick lay beside him within easy reach.

The moon was now high above the house. Through the open window they could see the comforting stars like friendly eyes watching in the sky. One by one the clocks of the town struck midnight, and when the sounds died away the deep silence of a windless night fell again over everything. Only the boom of the sea, far away and lugubrious, filled the air with hollow murmurs.

Inside the house the silence became awful; awful, he thought, because any minute now it might be broken by sounds portending terror. The strain of waiting told more and more severely on the nerves; they talked in whispers when they talked at all, for their voices aloud sounded queer and unnatural. A chilliness, not altogether due to the night air, invaded the room, and made them cold. The influences against them, whatever these might be were slowly robbing them of self-confidence, and the power of decisive action: their forces were on the wane, and the possibility of real fear took on a new and terrible meaning. He began to tremble for the elderly woman by his side, whose pluck could hardly save her beyond a certain extent.

He heard the blood singing in his veins. It sometimes seemed so loud that he fancied it prevented his hearing properly certain other sounds that were beginning very faintly to make themselves audible in the depths of the house. Every time he fastened his attention on these sounds, they instantly ceased. They certainly came no nearer. Yet he could not rid himself of the idea that movement was going on somewhere in the lower regions of the house. The drawing room floor, where the door had been so strangely closed, seemed too near; the sounds were further off than that. He thought of the great kitchen, with the scurrying black-beetles, and of the dismal little scullery; but, somehow or other, they did not seem to come from there either. Surely they were not *outside* the house!

Then, suddenly, the truth flashed into his mind, and for the space of a minute he felt as if his blood had stopped flowing and turned to ice.

The sounds were not downstairs at all; they were *upstairs*— upstairs, somewhere among those horrid gloomy little servants' rooms with their bits of broken furniture, low ceilings, and cramped windows—upstairs where the victim had first been disturbed and stalked to her death.

And the moment he discovered where the sounds were, he began to hear them more clearly. It was the sound of feet, moving stealthily along the passage overhead, in and out among the rooms, and past the furniture.

He turned quickly to steal a glance at the motionless figure seated beside him, to note whether she had shared his discovery. The faint candlelight coming through the crack in the cupboard door, threw her strongly-marked face into vivid relief against the white of the wall. But it was something else that made him catch his breath and stare again. An extraordinary something had come into her face and seemed to spread over her features like a mask; it smoothed out the deep lines and drew the skin everywhere a little tighter so that the wrinkles disappeared; it brought into the face— with the sole exception of the old eyes—an appearance of youth and almost of childhood.

He stared in speechless amazement—amazement that was dangerously near to horror. It was his aunt's face indeed, but it was her face of forty years ago, the vacant innocent face of a girl. He had heard stories of that strange effect of terror which could wipe a human countenance clean of other emotions, obliterating all previous expression; but he had never realized that it could be literally true, or could mean anything so simply horrible as what he now saw. For the dreadful signature of overmastering fear was written plainly in that utter vacancy of the girlish face beside him; and when, feeling his intense gaze, she turned to look at him, he instinctively closed his eyes tightly to shut out the sight.

Yet, when he turned a minute later, his feelings well in hand, he saw to his intense relief another expression; his aunt was smiling, and though the face was deathly white, the awful veil had lifted and the normal look was returning.

'Anything wrong?' was all he could think of to say at the moment. And the answer was eloquent, coming from such a woman.

'I feel cold—and a little frightened,' she whispered.

He offered to close the window, but she seized hold of him and begged him not to leave her side even for an instant.

'It's upstairs, I know,' she whispered, with an odd half laugh; 'but I can't possibly go up.'

But Shorthouse thought otherwise, knowing that in action lay their best hope of self-control.

He took the brandy flask and poured out a glass of neat spirit, stiff enough to help anybody over anything. She swallowed it with a little shiver. His only idea now was to get out of the house before her collapse became inevitable; but this could not safely be done by turning tail and running from the enemy. Inaction was no longer possible; every minute he was growing less master of himself, and desperate, aggressive measures were imperative without further delay. Moreover, the action must be taken *towards* the enemy, not away from it; the climax, if necessary and unavoidable, would have to be faced boldly. He could do it now; but in ten minutes he might not have the force left to act for himself, much less for both!

Upstairs, the sounds were meanwhile becoming louder and closer, accompanied by occasional creaking of the boards. Someone was moving stealthily about, stumbling now and then awkwardly against the furniture.

Waiting a few moments to allow the tremendous dose of spirits to produce its effect, and knowing this would last but a short time under the circumstances, Shorthouse then quietly got on his feet, saying in a determined voice—

'Now, Aunt Julia, we'll go upstairs and find out what all this noise is about. You must come too. It's what we agreed.'

He picked up his stick and went to the cupboard for the candle. A limp form rose shakily beside him breathing hard, and he heard a voice say very faintly something about being 'ready to come.' The woman's courage amazed him; it was so much greater than his own; and, as they advanced, holding aloft the dripping candle, some subtle force exhaled from this trembling, white-faced old woman at his side that was the true source of his inspiration. It held something really great that shamed him and gave him the support without which he would have proved far less equal to the occasion.

They crossed the dark landing, avoiding with their eyes the deep black space over the banisters. Then they began to mount the narrow staircase to meet the sounds which, minute by minute, grew louder and nearer. About halfway up the stairs Aunt Julia stumbled and Shorthouse turned to catch her by the arm, and just at that moment there came a terrific crash in the servants' corridor overhead. It was instantly followed by a shrill, agonized scream that was a cry of terror and a cry for help melted into one.

Before they could move aside, or go down a single step, someone came rushing along the passage overhead, blundering horribly, racing madly, at full speed, three steps at a time, down the very staircase where they stood. The steps were light and uncertain; but close behind them sounded the heavier tread of another person, and the staircase seemed to shake.

Shorthouse and his companion just had time to flatten themselves against the wall when the jumble of flying steps was upon them, and two persons, with the slightest possible interval between them, dashed past at full speed. It was a perfect whirlwind of sound breaking in upon the midnight silence of the empty building.

The two runners, pursuer and pursued, had passed clean through them where they stood, and already with a thud the boards below had received first one, then the other. Yet they had seen absolutely nothing—not a hand, or arm, or face, or even a shred of flying clothing.

There came a second's pause. Then the first one, the lighter of the two, obviously the pursued one, ran with uncertain footsteps into the little room which Shorthouse and his aunt had just left. The heavier one followed. There was a sound of scuffling, gasping, and smothered screaming; and then out on to the landing came the step—of a single person *treading weightily*.

A dead silence followed for the space of half a minute, and then was heard a rushing sound through the air. It was followed by a dull, crashing thud in the depths of the house below—on the stone floor of the hall.

Utter silence reigned after. Nothing moved. The flame of the candle was steady. It had been steady the whole time, and the air had been undisturbed by any movement whatsoever. Palsied with terror, Aunt Julia, without waiting for her companion, began fumbling her way downstairs; she was crying gently to herself, and when Shorthouse put his arm round her and half carried her he felt that she was trembling like a leaf. He went into the little room and picked up the cloak from the floor, and, arm in arm, walking very slowly, without speaking a word or looking once behind them, they marched down the three flights into the hall.

In the hall they saw nothing, but the whole way down the stairs they were conscious that someone followed them; step by step; when they went faster IT was left behind, and when they went more slowly IT caught them up. But never once did they look behind to see; and at each turning of the staircase they lowered their eyes for fear of the following horror they might see upon the stairs above.

With trembling hands Shorthouse opened the front door, and they walked out into the moonlight and drew a deep breath of the cool night air blowing in from the sea.

The Phantom 'Rickshaw

BY RUDYARD KIPLING

> May no ill dreams disturb my rest,
> Nor Powers of Darkness me molest.
>
> *Evening Hymn*

One of the few advantages that India has over England is a great Knowability. After five years' service a man is directly or indirectly acquainted with the two or three hundred Civilians in his Province, all the Messes of ten or twelve Regiments and Batteries, and some fifteen hundred other people of the non-official caste. In ten years his knowledge should be doubled, and at the end of twenty he knows, or knows something about, every Englishman in the Empire, and may travel anywhere and everywhere without paying hotel-bills.

Globetrotters who expect entertainment as a right, have, even within my memory, blunted this open-heartedness, but nonetheless today, if you belong to the Inner Circle and are neither a Bear nor a Black Sheep, all houses are open to you, and our small world is very, very kind and helpful.

Rickett of Kamartha stayed with Polder of Kumaon some fifteen years ago. He meant to stay two nights, but was knocked down by rheumatic fever, and for six weeks disorganized Polder's establishment, stopped Polder's work, and nearly died in Polder's bedroom. Polder behaves as though he had been placed under eternal obligation by Rickett, and yearly sends the little Ricketts a box of presents and toys. It is the same everywhere. The men who do not take the trouble to conceal from you their opinion that you are an incompetent ass, and the women who blacken your character and misunderstand your wife's amusements, will work themselves to the bone in your behalf if you fall sick or into serious trouble.

Heatherlegh, the Doctor, kept, in addition to his regular practice, a hospital on his private account—an arrangement of loose boxes for Incurables, his friend called it—but it was really a sort of fitting-up shed for craft that had been damaged by stress of weather. The weather in India is often sultry, and since the tale of bricks is always a fixed quantity, and the only liberty allowed is permission to work overtime and get no thanks, men occasionally breakdown and become as mixed as the metaphors in this sentence.

Heatherlegh is the dearest doctor that ever was, and his invariable prescription to all his patients is, 'Lie low, go slow, and keep cool.' He says that more men are killed by overwork than the importance of this world justifies. He maintains that overwork slew Pansay, who died under his hands about three years ago. He has, of course, the right to speak authoritatively, and he laughs at my theory that there was a crack in Pansay's head and a little bit of the Dark World came through and pressed him to death. 'Pansay went off the handle,' says Heatherlegh, 'after the stimulus of long leave at Home. He may or he may not have behaved like a blackguard to Mrs Keith-Wessington. My notion is that the work of the Katabundi Settlement ran him off his legs, and that he took to brooding and making much of an ordinary E & O. flirtation. He certainly was engaged to Miss Mannering, and she certainly broke off the engagement. Then he took a feverish chill and all that nonsense about ghosts developed. Overwork started his illness, kept it alight, and killed him, poor devil. Write him off to the System that uses one man to do the work of two and a half men.

I do not believe this. I use to sit up with Pansay sometimes when Heatherlegh was called out to patients and I happened to be within claim. The man would make me most unhappy by describing in a low, even voice, the procession that was always passing at the bottom of the bed. He had a sick man's command of language. When he recovered I suggested that he should write out the whole affair from beginning to end, knowing that ink might assist him to ease his mind.

He was in a high fever while he was writing, and the blood-and-thunder Magazine diction he adopted did not calm him. Two months afterwards he was reported fit for duty, but, in spite of the fact that he was urgently needed to help an undermanned Commission stagger through a deficit, he preferred to die; vowing at the last that he was hag-ridden. I got his manuscript before he died, and this is his version of the affair, dated 1885, exactly as he wrote it:—

My doctor tells me that I need rest and change of air. It is not improbable that I shall get both ere long—rest that neither the red-coated messenger nor the midday gun can break, and change of air far beyond that which any homeward-bound steamer can give me. In the meantime I am resolved to stay where I am; and, in flat defiance of my doctor's orders, to take all the world into my confidence. You shall learn for yourselves the precise nature of my malady, and shall, too, judge for yourselves whether any man born of woman on this weary earth was ever so tormented as I.

Speaking now as a condemned criminal might speak ere the drop-bolts are drawn, my story, wild and hideously improbable as it may appear, demands at least attention. That it will ever receive credence I utterly disbelieve. Two months ago I should have scouted as mad or drunk the man who had dared tell me the like. Two months ago I was the happiest man in India. Today from Peshawar to the sea, there is no one more wretched. My doctor and I are the only two who know this. His explanation is, that my brain, digestion, and eyesight are all slightly affected; giving rise to my frequent and persistent 'delusions.' Delusions, indeed I call him a fool; but he attends me still with the same unwearied smile, the same bland professional manner, the same neatly-trimmed red whiskers, till I begin to suspect that I am an ungrateful, evil-tempered invalid. But you shall judge for yourselves.

Three years ago it was my fortune—my great misfortune—to sail from Gravesend to Bombay, on return from long leave, with one Agnes Keith-Wessington, wife of an officer on the Bombay side. It does not in the least concern you to know what manner of woman she was. Be content with the knowledge that, ere the voyage had ended, both she and I were desperately and unreasoningly in love with one another. Heaven knows that I can make the admission now without one particle of vanity. In matters of this sort there is always one who gives and another who accepts. From the first day of our ill-omened attachment, I was conscious that Agnes's passion was a stronger, a more dominant, and—if I may use the expression—a purer sentiment than mine. Whether she recognized the fact then, I do not know. Afterwards it was bitterly plain to both of us.

Arrived at Bombay in the spring of the year, we went our respective ways, to meet no more for the next three or four months, when my leave and her love took us both to Simla. There we spent the season together, and there my fire of straw burnt itself out to a pitiful end with the closing year. I attempt no excuse. I make no apology. Mrs Wessington had given up much for my sake, and was prepared to give up all. From my own lips, in August 1882, she learnt that I was sick of her presence, tired of her company, and weary of the sound of her voice. Ninety-nine women out of a hundred would have wearied of me as I wearied of them; seventy-five of that number would have promptly avenged themselves by active and obtrusive flirtation with other men. Mrs Wessington was the hundredth. On her neither my openly-expressed aversion nor the cutting brutalities with which I garnished our interviews had the least effect.

'Jack, darling!' was her one eternal cuckoo cry: 'I'm sure it's all a mistake—a hideous mistake; and we'll be good friends again some day. *Please* forgive me, Jack, dear.'

I was the offender, and I knew it. That knowledge transformed my pity into passive endurance, and, eventually into blind hate—the same instinct, I suppose, which prompts a man to savagely stamp on the spider he has but half killed. And with this hate in my bosom the season of 1882 came to an end.

Next year we met again at Simla—she with her monotonous face and timid attempts at reconciliation, and I with loathing of her in every fibre of my frame. Several times I could not avoid meeting her alone; and on each occasion her words were identically the same. Still the unreasoning wail that it was all a 'mistake'; and still the hope of eventually 'making friends.' I might have seen, had I dared to look, that that hope only was keeping her alive. She grew more wan and thin month by month. You will agree with me, at least, that such conduct would have driven anyone to despair. It was uncalled for; childish; unwomanly. I maintain that she was much to blame. And again, sometimes, in the black, fever-stricken night-watches, I have begun to think that I might have been a little kinder to her. But that really *is* a delusion. I could not have continued pretending to love her when I didn't; could I? It would have been unfair to us both.

Last year we met again—on the same terms as before. The same weary appeals, and the same curt answers from my lips. At least I would make her see how wholly wrong and hopeless were her attempts at resuming the old relationship. As the season wore on, we fell apart—that is to say, she found it difficult to meet me, for I had other and more absorbing interests to attend to. When I think it over quietly in my sickroom, the season of 1884 seems a confused nightmare wherein light and shade were fantastically intermingled—my courtship of little Kitty Mannering; my hopes, doubts, and fears; our long rides together; my trembling avowal of attachment; her reply; and now and again a vision of a white face flitting by in the 'rickshaw with the black and white liveries I once watched for so earnestly; the wave of Mrs Wessington's gloved hand; and, when she met me alone, which was but seldom, the irksome monotony of her appeal. I loved Kitty Mannering; honestly, heartily loved her, and with my love for her grew my hatred for Agnes. In August Kitty and I were engaged. The next day I met those accursed 'magpie' *jhampanies* at the back of Jakko, and, moved by some passing sentiment of pity, stopped to tell Mrs Wessington everything. She knew it already.

'So I hear you're engaged, Jack dear.' Then, without a moment's pause: 'I'm sure it's all a mistake—a hideous mistake. We shall be as good friends some day Jack, as we ever were.'

My answer might have made even a man wince. It cut the dying woman before me like the blow of a whip. 'Please forgive me, Jack; I didn't mean to make you angry; but it's true, it's true!'

And Mrs Wessington broke down completely. I turned away and left her to finish her journey in peace, feeling, but only for a moment or two, that I had been an unutterably mean hound. I looked back, and saw that she had turned her 'rickshaw with the idea, I suppose, of overtaking me.

The scene and its surroundings were photographed on my memory. The rain-swept sky (we were at the end of the wet weather), the sodden, dingy pines, the muddy road, and the black powder-riven cliffs formed a gloomy background against which the black and white liveries of the *jhampanies*, the yellow-panelled 'rickshaw and Mrs Wessington's down-bowed golden head stood out clearly. She was holding her handkerchief in her left hand and was leaning back exhausted against the 'rickshaw cushions. I turned my horse up a bypath near the Sanjowlie Reservoir and literally ran away. Once I fancied I heard a faint call of Jack!' This may have been imagination. I never stopped to verify it. Ten minutes later I came across Kitty on horseback; and, in the delight of a long ride with her, forgot all about the interview.

A week later Mrs Wessington died, and the inexpressible burden of her existence was removed from my life. I went Plainsward perfectly happy. Before three months were over I had forgotten all about her, except that at times the discovery of some of her old letters reminded me unpleasantly of our bygone relationship. By January I had disinterred what was left of our correspondence from among my scattered belongings and had burnt it. At the beginning of April of this year, 1885, I was at Simla—semi-deserted Simla—once more, and was deep in lover's talks and walks with Kitty. It was decided that we should be married at the end of June. You will understand, therefore, that, loving Kitty as I did, I am not saying too much when I pronounce myself to have been, at that time, the happiest man in India.

Fourteen delightful days passed almost before I noticed their flight. Then, aroused to the sense of what was proper among mortals circumstanced as we were, I pointed out to Kitty that an engagement ring was the outward and visible sign of her dignity as an engaged girl; and that she must forthwith come to Hamilton's to be measured for one. Up to that moment, I give you my word, we had completely forgotten so trivial a matter. To Hamilton's we accordingly went on 15 April 1885. Remember that—whatever my doctor may say to the contrary—I was then in perfect health, enjoying a well-balanced mind and an *absolutely* tranquil spirit. Kitty and I entered Hamilton's shop together, and there, regardless of the order of affairs, I measured Kitty for the ring in the presence of the amused assistant. The ring was a sapphire with two diamonds. We then rode out down the slope that leads to the Combermere Bridge and Peliti's shop.

While my Waler was cautiously feeling his way over the loose shale, and Kitty was laughing and chattering at my side—while all Simla, that is to say as much of it as had then come from the Plains, was grouped round the reading-room and Peliti's veranda,—I was aware that someone, apparently at a vast distance, was calling me by my Christian name. It struck me that I had heard the voice before, but when and where I could not at once determine. In the short space it took to cover the road between the path from Hamilton's shop and the first plank of the Combermere Bridge I had thought over half a dozen people who might have committed such a solecism, and had eventually decided that it must have been some singing in my ears. Immediately opposite Peliti's shop my eye was arrested by the sight of *four jhampanies* in 'magpie' livery, pulling a yellow-panelled, cheap, bazar 'rickshaw. In a moment my mind flew back to the previous season and Mrs Wessington with a sense of irritation and disgust. Was it not enough that the woman was dead and done with, without her black and white servitors reappearing to spoil the day's happiness? Whoever employed them now I thought I would call upon, and ask as a personal favour to change her *jhamptmies'* livery I would hire die men myself, and, if necessary, buy their coats from off their backs. It is impossible to say here what a flood of undesirable memories their presence evoked.

'Kitty,' I cried, 'there are poor Mrs Wessington's *jhampanies* turned up again! I wonder who has them now?'

Kitty had known Mrs Wessington slightly last season, and had always been interested in the sickly woman.

'What? Where?' she asked. 'I can't see them anywhere.'

Even as she spoke, her horse, swerving from a laden mule, threw himself directly in front of the advancing 'rickshaw. I had scarcely time to utter a word of warning when to my unutterable horror, horse and rider passed *through* men and carriage as if they had been thin air.

'What's the matter?' cried Kitty; 'what made you call out so foolishly, Jack? If I *am* engaged I don't want all creation to know about it. There was lots of space between the mule and the veranda; and, if you think I can't ride—— There!'

Whereupon wilful Kitty set off, her dainty little head in the air, at a hand-gallop in the direction of the Band-stand; fully expecting, as she herself afterwards told me, that I should follow her. What was the matter? Nothing indeed. Either that I was mad or drunk, or that Simla was haunted with devils. 1 reined in my impatient Cob, and turned round. The 'rickshaw had turned too, and now stood immediately facing me, near the left railing of the Combermere Bridge.

'Jack! Jack, darling!' (There was no mistake about the words this time: they rang through my brain as if they had been shouted in my ear.) 'It's some hideous mistake, I'm sure. *Please* forgive me, Jack, and lets' be friends again.'

The 'rickshaw-hood had fallen back, and inside, as I hope and pray daily for the death I dread by night, sat Mrs Keith-Wessington, handkerchief in hand, and golden head bowed on her breast.

How long I stared motionless I do not know. Finally, I was aroused by my sais taking the Waler's bridle and asking whether I was ill. From the horrible to the commonplace is but a step. I tumbled off my horse and dashed, half fainting, into Peliti's for a glass of cherry-brandy. There two or three couples were gathered round the coffee-tables discussing the gossip of the day. Their trivialities were more comforting to me just then than the consolations of religion could have been. I plunged into the midst of the conversation at once; chatted, laughed, and jested with a face (when I caught a glimpse of it in a mirror) as white and drawn as that of a corpse. Three or four men noticed my condition; and, evidently setting it down to the results of over-many pegs, charitably endeavoured to draw me apart from the rest of the loungers. But I refused to be led away. I wanted the company of my kind—as a child rushes into the midst of the dinner-party after a fright in the dark. I must have talked for about ten minutes or so, though it seemed an eternity to me, when I heard Kitty's clear voice outside enquiring for me. In another minute she had entered the shop, prepared to upbraid me for failing so signally in my duties. Something in my face stopped her.

'Why, Jack,' she cried, 'what *have* you been doing? What *has* happened? Are you ill?' Thus driven into a direct lie, I said that the sun had been a little too much for me. It was close upon five o'clock of a cloudy April afternoon, and the sun had been hidden all day. I saw my mistake as soon as the words were out of my mouth: attempted to recover it; blundered hopelessly and followed Kitty, in a regal rage, out of doors, amid the smiles of my acquaintances. I made some excuse (I have forgotten what) on the score of my feeling faint; and cantered away to my hotel, leaving Kitty to finish the ride by herself.

In my room I sat down and tried calmly to reason out the matter. Here was I, Theobald Jack Pansay, a well-educated Bengal Civilian in the year of grace 1885, presumably sane, certainly healthy, driven in terror from my sweetheart's side by the apparition of a woman who had been dead and buried eight months ago. These were facts that I could not blink. Nothing was further from my thought than any memory of Mrs Wessington when Kitty and I left Hamilton's shop. Nothing was more utterly commonplace than the stretch of wall opposite Peliti's. It was broad daylight. The road was full of people; and yet here, look you, in defiance of every law of probability, in direct outrage of Nature's ordinance, there had appeared to me a face from the grave.

Kitty's Arab had gone *through* the 'rickshaw: so that my first hope that some woman marvellously like Mrs Wessington had hired the carriage and the coolies with their old livery was lost. Again and again I went round this treadmill of thought; and again and again gave up baffled and in despair. The voice was as inexplicable as the apparition. I had originally some wild notion of confiding it all to Kitty; of begging her to marry me at once; and in her arms defying the ghostly occupant of the 'rickshaw. 'After all,' I argued, 'the presence of the 'rickshaw is in itself enough to prove the existence of a spectral illusion. One may see ghosts of men and women, but surely never coolies and carriages. The whole thing is absurd. Fancy the ghost of a hillman!'

Next morning I sent a penitent note to Kitty imploring her to overlook my strange conduct of the previous afternoon. My Divinity was still very wroth, and a personal apology was necessary. I explained, with a fluency born of night-long pondering over a falsehood, that I had been attacked with a sudden palpitation of the heart—the result of indigestion. This eminently practical solution had its effect; and Kitty and I rode out that afternoon with the shadow of my first lie dividing us.

Nothing would please her save a canter round Jakko. With my nerves still unstrung from the previous night I feebly protested against the notion, suggesting Observatory Hill, Jutogh, the Boileaugunge road—anything rather than the Jakko round. Kitty was angry and a little hurt; so I yielded from fear of provoking further misunderstanding, and we set out together towards Chota Simla. We walked a greater part of the way, and, according to our custom, cantered from a mile or so below the Convent to the stretch of level road by the Sanjowlie Reservoir. The wretched horses appeared to fly, and my heart beat quicker and quicker as we neared the crest of the ascent. My mind had been full of Mrs Wessington all the afternoon; and every inch of the Jakko road bore witness to our old-time walks and talks. The bowlders were full of it; the pines sang it aloud overhead; the rain-fed torrents giggled and chuckled unseen over the shameful story; and the wind in my ears chanted the iniquity aloud.

As a fitting climax, in the middle of the level men call the Ladies' Mile the Horror was awaiting me. No other 'rickshaw was in sight-only the four black and white *jhampanies,* the yellow-panelled carriage, and the golden head of the woman within—all apparently just as I had left them eight months and one fortnight ago! For an instant I fancied that Kitty *must* see what I saw—we were so marvellously sympathetic in all things. Her next words undeceived me—'Not a soul in sight! Come along, Jack, and I'll race you to the Reservoir buildings!' Her wiry little Arab was off like a bird, my Waler following close behind, and in this order we dashed under the cliffs. Half a minute brought us within fifty yards of the 'rickshaw. I pulled my Waler and fell back a little. The 'rickshaw was directly in the middle of the road; and once more the Arab passed through it, my horse following. 'Jack! Jack dear! *Please* forgive me,' rang with a wail in my ears, and, after an interval: 'It's all a mistake, a hideous mistake!'

I spurred my horse like a man possessed. When I turned my head at the Reservoir works, the black and white liveries were still waiting—patiently waiting—under the grey hillside, and the wind brought me a mocking echo of the words I had just heard. Kitty bantered me a good deal on my silence throughout the remainder of the ride. I had been talking up till then wildly and at random. To save my life I could not speak afterwards naturally, and from Sanjowlie to the Church wisely held my tongue.

I was to dine with the Mannerings that night, and had barely time to canter home to dress. On the road to Elysium Hill I overheard two men talking together in the dusk.—'It's a curious thing,' said one, 'how completely all trace of it disappeared. You know my wife was insanely fond of the woman (never could see anything in her myself), and wanted me to pick up her old 'rickshaw and coolies if they were to be got for love or money. Morbid sort of fancy I call it; but I've got to do what the *Memsabib* tells me. Would you believe that the man she hired it from tells me that all four of the men—they were brothers—died of cholera on the way to Hardwar, poor devils;

and the 'rickshaw has been broken up by the man himself. 'Told me he never used a dead *Memsahib's* 'rickshaw. 'Spoilt his luck. Queer notion, wasn't it? Fancy poor little Mrs Wessington spoiling any one's luck except her own!' I laughed aloud at this point; and my laugh jarred on me as I uttered it. So there *were* ghosts of 'rickshaws after all, and ghostly employments in the other world! How much did Mrs Wessington give her men? What were their hours? Where did they go?

And for visible answer to my last question I saw the infernal Thing blocking my path in the twilight. The dead travel fast, and by short cuts unknown to ordinary coolies. I laughed aloud a second time and checked my laughter suddenly, for I was afraid I was going mad. Mad to a certain extent I must have been, for I recollect that I reined in my horse at the head of the 'rickshaw, and politely wished Mrs Wessington 'Good evening.' Her answer was one I knew only too well. I listened to the end; and replied that I had heard it all before, but should be delighted if she had anything further to say.; Some malignant devil stronger than I must have entered into me that evening, for I have a dim recollection of talking the commonplaces of the day for five minutes to the Thing in front of me.

'Mad as a hatter, poor devil—or drunk. Max, try and get him to come home.'

Surely *that* was not Mrs Wessington's voice! The two men had overheard me speaking to the empty air, and had returned to look after me. They were very kind and considerate, and from their words evidently gathered that I was extremely drunk. I thanked them confusedly and cantered away to my hotel, there changed, and arrived at the Mannerings' ten minutes late. I pleaded the darkness of the night as an excuse; was rebuked by Kitty for my unlover-like tardiness; and sat down.

The conversation had already become general; and under cover of it, I was addressing some tender small talk to my sweet-heart when I was aware that at the further end of the table a short red-whiskered man was describing, with much broidery, his encounter with a mad unknown that evening.

A few sentences convinced me that he was repeating the incident of half an hour ago. In the middle of the story he looked round for applause, as professional story-tellers do, caught my eye, and straightway collapsed. There was a moment's awkward silence, and the red-whiskered man muttered something to the effect that he had 'forgotten the rest,' thereby sacrificing a reputation as a good story-teller which he had built up for six seasons past. I blessed him from the bottom of my heart, and—went on with my fish.

In the fulness of time that dinner came to an end; and with genuine regret I tore myself away from Kitty—as certain as I was of my own existence that it would be waiting for me outside the door. The red-whiskered man, who had been introduced to me as Dr Heatherlegh of Simla, volunteered to bear me company as far as our roads lay together. I accepted his offer with gratitude.

My instinct had not deceived me. It lay in readiness in the Mall, and, in what seemed devilish mockery of our ways, with a lighted head lamp. The red-whiskered man went to the point at once, in a manner that showed he had been thinking over it all dinner-time.

'I say, Pansay, what the deuce was the matter with you this evening on the Elysium Road?' The suddenness of the question wrenched an answer from me before I was aware.

'That!' said I, pointing to it.

'*That* may be either D.T. or eyes for aught I know. Now you don't liquor. I saw as much at dinner, so it can't be D.T. There's nothing whatever where you're pointing, though you're sweating and trembling with fright, like a scared pony. Therefore, I conclude that it's eyes. And I ought to understand all about them. Come along home with me. I'm on the Blessington lower road.'

To my intense delight the 'rickshaw instead of waiting for us kept about twenty yards ahead—and this, too, whether we walked, trotted, or cantered. In the course of that long night ride I had told my companion almost as much as I have told you here.

'Well, you've spoilt one of the best tales I've ever laid tongue to,' said he, 'but I'll forgive you for the sake of what you've gone through. Now come home and do what I tell you; and when I've cured you, young man, let this be a lesson to you to steer clear of women and indigestible food till the day of your death.'

The 'rickshaw kept steady in front; and my red-whiskered friend seemed to derive great pleasure from my account of its exact whereabouts.

'Eyes, Pansay—all eyes, brain, and stomach. And the greatest of these three is stomach. You've too much conceited brain, too little stomach, and thoroughly unhealthy eyes. Get your stomach straight and the rest follows. And all that's French for a liver pill. I'll take sole medical charge of you from this hour! For you're too interesting a phenomenon to be passed over.'

By this time we were deep in the shadow of the Blessington lower road and the 'rickshaw came to a dead stop under a pine-clad, overhanging shale cliff. Instinctively I halted too, giving my reason. Heatherlegh rapped out an oath.

'Now, if you think I'm going to spend a cold night on the hillside for the sake of a stomach-*cum*-brain-*cum*-eye illusion——Lord, ha' mercy! What's that?'

There was a muffled report, a blinding smother of dust just in front of us, a crack, the noise of rent boughs, and about ten yards of the cliff side—pines, undergrowth, and all—slid down into the road below, completely blocking it up. The uprooted trees swayed and tottered for a moment like drunken giants in the gloom, and then fell prone among their fellows with a thunderous crash. Our two horses stood motionless and sweating with fear. As soon as the rattle of falling earth and stone had subsided, my companion muttered: 'Man, if we'd gone forward we should have been ten feet deep in our graves by now. "There are more things in heaven and earth" ... Come home, Pansay and thank God. I want a peg badly.'

We retraced our way over the Church Ridge, and I arrived at Dr Heatherlegh's house shortly after midnight.

His attempts towards my cure commenced almost immediately, and for a week I never left his sight. Many a time in the course of that week did I bless the good-fortune which had thrown me in contact with Simla's best and kindest doctor. Day by day my spirits grew lighter and more equable. Day by day, too, I became more and more inclined to fall in with Heatherlegh's 'spectral illusion' theory implicating eyes, brain, and stomach. I wrote to Kitty, telling her that a slight sprain caused by a fall from my horse kept me indoors for a few days; and that I should be recovered before she had time to regret my absence.

Heatherlegh's treatment was simple to a degree. It consisted of liver pills, cold-water baths, and strong exercise, taken in the dusk or at early dawn,—for, as he sagely observed: 'A man with a sprained ankle doesn't walk a dozen miles a day and your young woman might be wondering if she saw you.'

At the end of the week, after much examination of pupil and pulse, and strict injunctions as to diet and pedestrianism, Heatherlegh dismissed me as brusquely as he had taken charge of me. Here is his parting benediction: 'Man, I certify to your mental cure, and that's as much as to say I've cured most of your bodily ailments. Now, get your traps out of this as soon as you can; and be off to make love to Miss Kitty.'

I was endeavouring to express my thanks for his kindness. He cut me short.

'Don't think I did this because I like you. I gather that you've behaved like a blackguard all through. But, all the same, you're a phenomenon, and as queer a phenomenon as you are a blackguard. No!'—checking me a second time—'not a rupee, please. Go out and see if you can find the eyes-brain-and-stomach business again. I'll give you a lakh for each time you see it.'

Half an hour later I was in the Mannerings' drawing room with Kitty—drunk with the intoxication of present happiness and the foreknowledge that I should never more be troubled with its hideous presence. Strong in the sense of my newfound security, I proposed a ride at once; and, by preference, a canter round Jakko.

Never had I felt so well, so overladen with vitality and mere animal spirits, as I did on the afternoon of 30 April. Kitty was delighted at the change in my appearance, and complimented me on it in her delightfully frank and outspoken manner. We left the Mannerings' house together, laughing and talking, and cantered along the Chota Simla road as of old.

I was in haste to reach the Sanjowlie Reservoir and there make my assurance doubly sure. The horses did their best, but seemed all too slow to my impatient mind. Kitty was astonished at my boisterousness. 'Why, Jack!' she cried at last, 'you are behaving like a child. What are you doing?'

We were just below the Convent, and from sheer wantonness I was making my Waler plunge and curvet across the road as I tickled it with the loop of my riding-whip.

'Doing?' I answered; 'nothing, dear. That's just it. If you'd been doing nothing for a week except lie up, you'd be as riotous as I.'

'Singing and murmuring in your feastful mirth,
    Joying to feel yourself alive;
Lord over Nature, Lord of the visible Earth,
    Lord of the senses five.'

My quotation was hardly out of my lips before we had rounded the corner above the Convent; and a few yards further on could see across to Sanjowhe. In the centre of the level road stood the black and white leveries, the yellow-panelled 'rickshaw; and Mrs Keith-Wessington. I pulled up, looked, rubbed my eyes, and, I believe, must have said something. The next thing I knew was that I was lying face downward on the road, with Kitty kneeling above me in tears.

'Has it gone, child?' I gasped. Kitty only wept more bitterly.

'Has what gone, Jack dear? What does it all mean? There must be a mistake somewhere, Jack. A hideous mistake.' Her last words brought me to my feet—mad—raving for the time being.

'Yes, there *is* a mistake somewhere,' I repeated, 'a hideous mistake. Come and look at It.'

I have an indistinct idea that I dragged Kitty by the wrist along the road up to where It stood, and implored her for pity's sake to speak to It; to tell It that we were betrothed; that neither Death nor Hell could break the tie between us: and Kitty only knows how much more to the same effect. Now and again I appealed passionately to the Terror in the 'rickshaw to bear witness to all I had said, and to release me from a torture that was killing me. As I talked I suppose I must have told Kitty of my old relations with Mrs Wessington, for I saw her listen intently with white face and blazing eyes.

'Thank you, Mr Pansay,' she said, 'that's *quite enough. Sais, ghora lao.'*

The sais, impassive as Orientals always are, had come up with the recaptured horses; and as Kitty sprang into her saddle I caught hold of her bridle, entreating her to hear me out and forgive. My answer was the cut of her riding-whip across my face from mouth to eye, and a word or two of farewell that even now I cannot write down. So I Judged and judged rightly, that Kitty knew all; and I staggered back to the side of the 'rickshaw. My face was cut and bleeding, and the blow of the riding-whip had raised a livid blue wheal on it. I had no self-respect. Just then, Heatherlegh, who must have been following Kitty and me at a distance, cantered up.

'Doctor,' I said, pointing to my face, 'here's Miss Mannering's signature to my order of dismissal and—— I'll thank you for that lakh as soon as convenient.'

Heatherlegh's face, even in my abject misery, moved me to laughter.

'I'll stake my professional reputation——' he began.

'Don't be a fool,' I whispered. 'I've lost my life's happiness and you'd better take me home.'

As I spoke the 'rickshaw was gone. Then I lost all knowledge of what was passing. The crest of Jakko seemed to heave and roll like the crest of a cloud and fall in upon me.

Seven days later (on 7 May, that is to say) I was aware that I was lying in Heatherlegh's room as weak as a little child. Heatherlegh was watching me intently from behind the papers on his writing-table. His first words were not encouraging; but I was too far spent to be much moved by them.

'Here's Miss Kitty has sent back your letters. You corresponded a good deal, you young people. Here's a packet that looks like a ring and a cheerful sort of a note from Mannering Papa, which I've taken the liberty of reading and burning. The old gentleman's not pleased with you.'

'And Kitty?' I asked dully.

'Rather more drawn than her father from what she says. By the same token you must have been letting out any number of queer reminiscences just before I met you. "Says that a man who would have behaved to a woman as you did to Mrs Wessington ought to kill himself out of sheer pity for his kind. She's a hot-headed little virago, your mash, "Will have it too that you were suffering from *D.T.* when that row on the Jakko road turned up. "Says she'll die before she ever speaks to you again.'

I groaned and turned over on the other side.

'Now you've got your choice, my friend. This engagement has to be broken off; and the Mannerings don't want to be too hard on you. Was it broken through *D.T.* or epileptic fits? Sorry I can't offer you a better exchange unless you'd prefer hereditary insanity. Say the word and I'll tell 'em it's fits. All Simla knows about that scene on the Ladies' Mile. Come! I'll give you five minutes to think over it.'

During those five minutes I believe that I explored thoroughly the lowest circles of the Inferno which it is permitted man to tread on earth. And at the same time I myself was watching myself faltering through the dark labyrinths of doubt, misery, and utter despair. I wondered, as Heatherlegh in his chair might have wondered, which dreadful alternative I should adopt. Presently I heard myself answering in a voice that I hardly recognized—

'They're confoundedly particular about morality in these parts. Give 'em fits, Heatherlegh, and my love. Now let me sleep a bit longer.'

Then my two selves joined, and it was only I (half crazed, devil-driven I) that tossed in my bed tracing step by step the history of the past month.

'But I am in Simla,' I kept repeating to myself. 'I, Jack Pansay, am in Simla, and there are no ghosts here. It's unreasonable of that woman to pretend there are. Why couldn't Agnes have left me alone? I never did her any harm. It might just as well have been me as Agnes. Only 'd never have come back on purpose to kill *her*. Why can't I be left done—left alone and happy?'

It was high noon when I first awoke: and the sun was low in the sky before I slept—slept as the tortured criminal sleeps on his rack, do worn to feel further pain.

Next day I could not leave my bed. Heatherlegh told me in the morning that he had received an answer from Mr Mannering, and that, thanks to his (Heatherlegh's) friendly offices, the story of my affliction had travelled through the length and breadth of Simla, where I was on all sides much pitied.

'And that's rather more than you deserve,' he concluded pleasantly, 'though the Lord knows you've been going through a pretty severe mill. Never mind; we'll cure you yet, you perverse phenomenon.'

I declined firmly to be cured. 'You've been much too good to me already, old man,' said I; 'but I don't think I need trouble you further.' In my heart I knew that nothing Heatherlegh could do would lighten the burden that had been laid upon me.

With that knowledge came also a sense of hopeless, impotent rebellion against the unreasonableness of it all. There were scores of men no better than I whose punishments had at least been reserved for another world; and I felt that it was bitterly, cruelly unfair that I alone should have been singled out for so hideous a fate. This mood would in time give place to another where it seemed that the 'rickshaw and I were the only realities in a world of shadows; that Kitty was a ghost; that Mannering. Heatherlegh, and all the other men and women I knew were all ghosts; and the great, grey hills themselves but vain shadows devised to torture me. From mood to mood I tossed backwards and forwards for seven weary days; my body growing daily stronger and stronger, until the bedroom looking-glass told me that I had returned to everyday life, and was as other men once more. Curiously enough my face showed no signs of the struggle I had gone through. It was pale indeed, but as expressionless and commonplace as ever. I had expected some permanent alteration—visible evidence of the disease that was eating me away. I found nothing.

On 15 May I left Heatherlegh's house at eleven o'clock in the morning; and the instinct of the bachelor drove me to the Club.

There I found that every man knew my story as told by Heatherlegh, and was, in clumsy fashion, abnormally kind and attentive. Nevertheless, I recognized that for the rest of my natural life I should be among but not of my fellows; and I envied very bitterly indeed the laughing coolies on the Mall below. I lunched at the Club, and at four o'clock wandered aimlessly down the Mall in the vague hope of meeting Kitty, Close to the Band-stand the black and white liveries joined me; and I heard Mrs Wessington's old appeal at my side. I had been expecting this ever since I came out; and was only surprised at her delay. The phantom 'rickshaw and I went side by side along the Chota Simla road in silence. Close to the bazar, Kitty and a man on horseback overtook and passed us. For any sign she gave I might have been a dog in the road. She did not even pay me the compliment of quickening her pace; though the rainy afternoon had served for an excuse.

So Kitty and her companion, and I and my ghosdy Light-o'-Love, crept round Jakko in couples. The road was streaming with water; the pines dripped like roof-pipes on the rocks below, and the air was full of fine, driving rain. Two or three times I found myself saying to myself almost aloud: I'm Jack Pansay on leave at Simla—*at Simla!* Everyday, ordinary Simla. I mustn't forget that—I mustn't forget that.' Then I would try to recollect some of the gossip I had heard at the Club: the prices of So-and-So's horses—anything, in fact, that related to the work-a-day Anglo-Indian world I knew so well. I even repeated the multiplication-table rapidly to myself, to make quite sure that I was not taking leave of my senses. It gave me much comfort; and must have prevented my hearing Mrs Wessington for a time.

Once more I wearily climbed the Convent slope and entered the level road. Here Kitty and the man started off at a canter, and I was left alone with Mrs Wessington. 'Agnes,' said I, 'will you put back your hood and tell me what it all means?' The hood dropped noiselessly, and I was face to face with my dead and buried mistress. She was wearing the dress in which I had last seen her alive; carried the same tiny handkerchief in her right hand; and the same card-case in her left. (A woman eight months dead with a card-case!) I had to pin myself down to the multiplication-table, and to set both hands on the stone parapet of the road, to assure myself that that at least was real.

'Agnes,' I repeated, 'for pity's sake tell me what it all means.' Mrs Wessington leaned forward, with that odd, quick turn of the head I used to know so well, and spoke.

If my story had not already so madly overleaped the bounds of all human belief I should apologize to you now. As I know that no one—no, not even Kitty for whom it is written as some sort of justification of my conduct—will believe me, I will go on. Mrs Wessington spoke and I walked with her from the Sanjowlie road to the turning below the Commander-in-Chief's house as I might walk by the side of any living woman's 'rickshaw, deep in conversation. The second and most tormenting of my moods of sickness had suddenly laid hold upon me, and like the prince in Tennyson's poem, 'I seemed to move amid a world of ghosts.' There had been a garden-party at the Commander-in-Chief's, and we two joined the crowd of homeward-bound folk. As I saw them it seemed that *they* were the shadows—impalpable fantastic shadows—that divided for Mrs Wessington's 'rickshaw to pass through. What we said during the course of that weird interview I cannot—indeed, I dare not—tell. Heatherlegh's comment would have been a short laugh and a remark that I had been 'mashing a brain-eye-and-stomach chimera.' It was a ghastly and yet in some indefinable way a marvellously dear experience. Could it be possible, I wondered, that I was in this life to woo a second time the woman I had killed by my own neglect and cruelty?

I met Kitty on the homeward road—a shadow among shadows.

If I were to describe all the incidents of the next fortnight in their order, my story would never come to an end; and your patience would be exhausted. Morning after morning and evening after evening the ghostly 'rickshaw and I used to wander through Simla together. Wherever I went the four black and white liveries followed me and bore me company to and from my hotel. At the Theatre I found them amid the crowd of yelling *jhampanies;* outside the Club veranda, after a long evening of whist; at the Birthday Ball, waiting patinetly for my reappearance; and in broad daylight when I went calling. Save that it cast no shadow, the 'rickshaw was in every respect as real to look upon as one of wood and iron. More than once, indeed, I have had to check myself from warning some hard-riding friend against cantering over it. More than once I have walked down the Mall deep in conversation with Mrs Wessington to the unspeakable amazement of the passers-by.

Before I had been out and about a week I learned that the 'fit' theory had been discarded in favour of insanity. However, I made no change in my mode of life. I called, rode, and dined out as freely as ever. I had a passion for the society of my kind which I had never felt before; I hungered to be among the realities of life; and at the same time I felt vaguely unhappy when I had been separated too long from my ghostly companion. It would be almost impossible to describe my varying moods from 15 May up to today.

The presence of the 'rickshaw filled me by turns with horror, blind fear, a dim sort of pleasure, and utter despair. I dared not leave Simla; and I knew that my stay there was killing me. I knew, moreover, that it was my destiny to die slowly and a little everyday. My only anxiety was to get the penance over as quietly as might be. Alternately I hungered for a sight of Kitty and watched her outrageous flirtations with my successor—to speak more accurately, my successors—with amused interest. She was as much out of my life as I was out of hers. By day I wandered with Mrs Wessington almost content. By night I implored Heaven to let me return to the world as I used to know it. Above all these varying moods lay the sensation of dull, numbing wonder that the seen and the unseen should mingle so strangely on this earth to hound one poor soul to its grave.

★

27 August.—Heatherlegh has been indefatigable in his attendance on me; and only yesterday told me that I ought to send in an application for sick leave. An application to escape the company of a phantom! A request that the Government would graciously permit me to get rid of five ghosts and an airy 'rickshaw by going to England! Heatherlegh's proposition moved me to almost hysterical laughter. I told him that I should await the end quietly at Simla; and I am sure that the end is not far off. Believe me that I dread its advent more than any word can say; and I torture myself nightly with a thousand speculations as to the manner of my death.

Shall I die in my bed decently and as an English gentleman should die; or, in one last walk on the Mall, will my soul be wrenched from me to take its place for ever and ever by the side of that ghastly phantasm? Shall I return to my old lost allegiance in the next world, or shall I meet Agnes loathing her and bound to her side through all eternity? Shall we two hover over the scene of our lives till the end of Time? As the day of my death draws nearer, the intense horror that all living flesh feels toward escaped spirits from beyond the grave grows more and more powerful. It is an awful thing to go down quick among the dead with scarcely one-half of our life completed. It is a thousand times more awful to wait as I do in your midst, for I know not what unimaginable terror. Pity me, at least on the score of my 'delusion,' for I know you will never believe what I have written here. Yet as surely as ever a man was done to death by the Powers of Darkness, I am that man.

In justice, too, pity her. For as surely as ever woman was killed by man, I killed Mrs Wessington. And the last portion of my punishment is even now upon me.

Boomerang

BY OSCAR COOK

Warwick threw himself into a chair beside me, hitched up his trousers, and, leaning across, tapped me on the knee. 'You remember the story about Mendingham which you told me?' he asked.

I nodded. I was not likely to forget that affair.

'Well,' he went on, 'I've got as good a one to tell you. Had it straight from the filly's mouth, so to speak—and it's red-hot.'

I edged away in my chair, for there was something positively ghoulish in his delight, in the coarse way which he referred to a woman, and one who, if my inference were correct, must have known tragedy. But there is no stopping Warwick: he knows or admits no finer feelings or shame when his thirst for 'copy' is aroused. Like the litde boy in the well-known picture, 'he won't be happy till he's 'quenched' it'.

I ordered drinks, and when they had been served and we were alone, bade him get on with his sordid story.

'It's a wild tale,' he began, 'of two planter fellows in the interior of Borneo—and, as usual, there's a woman.'

'*The* woman?' I could not refrain from asking, thinking of his earlier remark.

'The same,' he replied. 'A veritable golden-haired filly, only her mane is streaked with grey and there's a great livid scar or weal right round her neck. She's the wife of Leopold Thring. The other end of the triangle is Clifford Macy.'

'And where do you come in?' I inquired.

Warwick closed one eye and pursed his lips.

'As a spinner of yams,' he answered sententiously. Then, with a return to his usual cynicism, 'The filly is down and out, but for some silly religious scruples feels she must live. I bought the story, therefore, after verifying the facts. Shall I go on?'

I nodded, for I must admit I was genuinely interested. The eternal triangle always intrigues: set in the wilds of Borneo it promised a variation of incident unusually refreshing in these sophisticated days. Besides, that scar was eloquent.

Warwick chuckled.

'The two men were partners,' he went on, 'on a small experimental estate far up in the interior. They had been at it for six years and were just about to reap the fruits of their labours very handsomely. Incidentally, Macy had been out in the Colony the full six years—and the strain was beginning to tell. Thring had been home eighteen months before, and on coming back had brought his bride, Rhona.

'That was the beginning of the trouble. It split up the partnership: brought in a new element: meant the building of a new bungalow.'

'For Macy?' I asked.

'Yes. And he didn't take kindly to it. He had got set. And then there was the loneliness of night after night alone, while the others—you understand?'

I nodded.

'Well,' Warwick continued, 'the expected happened. Macy flirted, philandered, and then fell violently in love. He was one of those fellows who never do things by halves. If he drank, he'd get fighting drunk: if he loved, he went all out on it: if he hated—well, hell was let loose.'

'And—Mrs Thring?' I queried, for it seemed to me that she might have a point of view.

'Fell between two stools—as so many women of a certain type do. She began by being just friendly and kind—you know the sort of thing—cheering the lonely man up, drifted into woman's eternal game of flirting, and then began to grow a little afraid of the fire she'd kindled. Too late she realized that she couldn't put the fire out—either hers or Macy's—and all the while she clung to some hereditary religious scruples.

'Thring was in many ways easygoing, but at the same time possessed of a curiously intense strain of jealous possessiveness. He was generous, too. If asked, he would share or give away his last shirt or crust. But let him think or feel that his rights or dues were being curtailed or taken and—well, he was a tough customer of rather primitive ideas.

'Rhona—that's the easiest way to think of the filly—soon found she was playing a game beyond her powers. Hers was no poker face, and Thring began to sense that something was wrong. She couldn't dissemble, and Macy made no attempt to hide his feelings. He didn't make it easy for her, and I guess from what the girl told me, life about this time was for her a sort of glorified hell—a suspicious husband on one hand, and an impetuous, devil-may-care lover on the other. She was living on a volcano.'

'Which might explode any minute,' I quietly said.

Warwick nodded.

'Exactly; or whenever Thring chose to spring the mine. He held the key to the situation, or, should I say, the time-fuse? The old story, but set in a primitive land full of possibilities. You've got me?'

For answer I offered Warwick a cigarette, and, taking one myself, lighted both.

'So far,' I said, 'with all your journalistic skill you've not got off the beaten track. Can't you improve?'

He chuckled, blew a cloud of smoke, and once again tapped my knee in his irritating manner.

'Your cynicism,' he countered, 'is but a poor cloak for your curiosity. In reality you're jumping mad to know the end, eh?'

I made no reply, and he went on.

'Well, matters went on from day to day till Rhona became worn to the proverbial shadow. Thring wanted to send her home, but she wouldn't go. She owed a duty to her husband: she couldn't bear to be parted from her lover, and she didn't dare leave the two men alone. She was terribly, horribly afraid.

'Macy grew more and more openly amorous and less restrained. Thring watched whenever possible with the cunning of an iguana. Then came a rainy, damp spell that tried nerves to the uttermost and the inevitable stupid little disagreements between Rhona and Thring—mere trifles, but enough to let the lid off. He challenged her——'

'And she?' I could not help asking, for Warwick has, I must admit, the knack of keeping one on edge.

'Like a blithering but sublime little idiot admitted that it was all true.'

For nearly a minute I was speechless. Somehow, although underneath I had expected Rhona to behave so, it seemed such a senseless, unbelievable thing to do. Then at last I found my voice.

'And Thring?' I said simply.

Warwick emptied his glass at a gulp.

'That's the most curious thing in the whole yarn,' he answered slowly. 'Thring took it as quietly as a lamb.'

'Stunned?' I suggested.

'That's what Rhona thought: what Macy believed when Rhona told him what had happened. In reality he must have been burning mad, a mass of white-hot revenge controlled by a devilish, cunning brain: he waited. A scene or a fight—and Macy was a big man— would have done no good. He would get his own back in his own time and in his own way. Meanwhile, there was the lull before the storm.

'Then, as so often happens, fate played a hand. Macy went sick with malaria—really ill—and even lining had to admit the necessity for Rhona to nurse him practically night and day. Macy owned his eventual recovery to her care, but even so his convalescence was a long job. In the end Rhona too crocked up through overwork, and Thring had them both on his hands. This was an opportunity better than he could have planned—it separated the lovers and gave him complete control.

'Obviously the time was ripe, ripe for Thring to score his revenge.

'The rains were over, the jungle had ceased wintering, and spring was in the air. The young grass and vegetation were shooting into new life: concurrently all the creepy, crawly insect life of the jungle and estate was young and vigorous and hungry too. These facts gave Thring the germ of an idea which he was not slow to perfect—an idea as devilish as man could devise.'

Warwick paused to press out the stub of his cigarette, and noticing that even he seemed affected by his recital, I prepared myself as best I could for a really gruesome horror. All I said, however, was, 'Go on.'

'It seems,' he continued, 'that in Borneo there is a kind of mammoth earwig—a thing almost as fine and gossamer as a spider's web, as long as a good-sized caterpillar, that lives on waxy secretions. These are integral parts of some flowers and trees, and lie buried deep in their recesses. It is one of the terrors of these particular tropics, for it moves and rests so lightly on a human being that one is practically unconscious of it, while, like its English relation, it has a decided liking for the human ear: on account of man's carnivorous diet, the wax in this has a strong and very succulent taste.'

As Warwick gave me those details, he sat upright on the edge of his easy-chair. He spoke slowly, emphasizing each point by hitting the palm of his left hand with the clenched fist of his right. It was impossible not to see the drift and inference of his remarks.

'You mean——?' I began.

'Exactly,' he broke in quickly, blowing a cloud of smoke from a fresh cigarette which he had nervously lighted. 'Exactly. It was a devilish idea. To put the giant earwig on Macy's hair just above the ear.'

'And then...?' I knew the famousness of the question, but speech relieved the growing sense of ticklish horror that was creeping over me.

'Do nothing. But rely on the filthy insect running true to type. Once in Macy's ear, it was a thousand-to-one chance against it ever coming out the same way: it would not be able to turn: to back out would be almost an impossibility, and so, feeding as it went, it would crawl right across inside his head, with the result that——'

The picture Warwick was drawing was more than I could bear: even my imagination, dulled by years of legal dry-as-dust affairs, saw and sickened at the possibilities. I put out a hand and gripped Warwick's arm.

'Stop, man!' I cried hoarsely. 'For God's sake, don't say any more. I understand. My God, but the man Thring must be a fiend!'

Warwick looked at me, and I saw that even his face had paled.

'Was,' he said meaningly. 'Perhaps you're right, perhaps he *was* a fiend. Yet, remember, Macy stole his wife.'

'But a torture like that! The deliberate creation of a living torment that would grow into madness. Warwick, you can't condone that!'

He looked at me for a moment and then slowly spread out his hands.

'Perhaps you're right,' he admitted. 'It was a bit thick, I know. But there's more to come.'

I closed my eyes and wondered if I could think of an excuse for leaving Warwick; but in spite of my real horror, my curiosity won the day.

'Get on with it,' I muttered, and leant back, eyes still shut, hands clenched. With teeth gritted together as if I myself were actually suffering the pain of that earwig slowly, daily creeping farther into and eating my brain, I waited.

Warwick was not slow to obey.

'I have told you,' he said, 'that Rhona had to nurse Macy, and even when he was better, though still weak, Thring insisted on her looking after him, though now he himself came more often.

'One afternoon Rhona was in Macy's bungalow alone with him: the house-boy was out. Rhona was on the veranda: Macy was asleep in the bedroom. Dusk was just falling: bats were flying about: the flying foxes, heavy with fruit, were returning home: the inevitable house rats were scurrying about the floors: the lamps had not been lit. An eerie, devastating hour. Rhona dropped some needlework and fought back tears. Then from the bedroom came a shriek. 'My head! My ear! Oh, God! My ear! Oh, God! The pain!'

'That was the beginning. The earwig had got well inside. Rhona rushed in and did all she could. Of course, there was nothing to see. Then for a little while Macy would be quiet because the earwig was quiet, sleeping or gorged. Then the vile thing would move or feed again, and Macy once more would shriek with the pain.

'And so it went on, day by day. Alternate quiet and alternate pain, each day for Macy, for Rhona a hell of nerve-rending expectancy. Waiting, always waiting for the pain that crept and crawled and twisted and writhed and moved slowly ever slowly, through and across Macy's brain.'

Warwick paused so long that I was compelled to open my eyes. His face was ghastly. Fortunately I could not see my own.

'And Thring?' I asked.

'Came often each day. Pretended sorrow and served out spurious dope—Rhona found the coloured water afterwards. He cleverly urged that Macy should be carried down to the coast for medical treatment, knowing full well that he was too ill and worn to bear the smallest strain. Then when Macy was an utter wreck, broken completely in mind and body, with hollow, hunted eyes, with ever-twitching fingers, with a body no part of which he could properly control or keep still, the earwig came out—at the other ear.

'As it happened, both Thring and Rhona were present. Macy must have suffered an excruciating pain, followed as usual by a period of quiescence: then, feeling a slight ticklish sensation on his cheek, put up his hand to rub or scratch. His fingers came in contact with the earwig and its fine gossamer hairs. Instinct did the rest. You follow?'

My tongue was still too dry to enable me to speak. Instead I nodded, and Warwick went on.

'He naturally was curious and looked to see what he was holding. In an instant he realized. Even Rhona could not be in doubt. The hairs were faintly but unmistakably covered here and there with blood, with wax and with grey matter.

'For a moment there was absolute silence between the three. At last Macy spoke.

' 'My God!' he just whispered. 'Oh, my God! What an escape!'

'Rhona burst into tears. Only Thring kept silent, and that was his mistake. The silence worried Macy, weak though he was. He looked from Rhona to Thring, and at the critical moment Thring could not meet his gaze. The truth was out. With an oath Macy threw the insect, now dead from the pressure of his fingers, straight into Thring's face. Then he crumpled up in his chair and sobbed and sobbed till even the chair shook.'

Again Warwick paused till I thought he would never go on. I had heard enough, I'll admit, and yet it seemed to me that at least there should be an epilogue.

'Is that all?' I tentatively asked.

Warwick shook his head.

'Nearly, but not quite,' he said. 'Rhona had ceased weeping and kept her eyes fixed on Thring—she dared not go and comfort Macy now. She saw him examine the dead earwig, having picked it up from the floor to which it had fallen, turn it this way and that, then produce from a pocket a magnifying-glass which he used daily for the inspection and detection of leaf disease on certain of the plants. As she watched, she saw the fear and disappointment leave his face, to be replaced by a look of cunning and evil satisfaction. Then for the first time he spoke.

' "Macy!" he called, in a sharp, loud voice.

Macy looked up.

'Thring held up the earwig. "This is dead now," he said—"dead. As dead as my friendship for you, you swine of a thief, as dead as my love for that whore who was my wife. It's dead, I tell you, dead, but it's a female. D'you get me? A female, and a female lays eggs, and before it died it——"

'He never finished. His baiting at last roused Macy, endowing him with the strength of madness and despair. With one spring he was at Thring's throat, bearing him down to the ground. Over and over they rolled on the floor, struggling for possession of the great hunting-knife stuck in Thring's belt. One moment Macy was on top, the next, Thring. Their breath and oaths came in great trembling gasps. They kicked and bit and scratched. And all the while Rhona watched, fascinated and terrified. Then Thring got definitely on top. He had one hand on Macy's throat, both knees on his chest, and with his free hand he was feeling for the knife. In that instant Rhona's religious scruples went by the board. She realized she only loved Macy, that her husband didn't count. She rushed to Macy's help. Thring saw her coming and let drive a blow at her head which almost stunned her. She fell on top of him just as he was whipping out the knife. Its edge caught her neck. The sudden spurt of blood shot into Thring's eyes, and blinded him. It was Macy's last chance. He knew it, and he took it.

'When Rhona came back to consciousness, Thring was dead, Macy was standing beside the body, which was gradually swelling to huge proportions as he worked, weakly but steadily, at the white ant exterminator pump, the nozzle of which was pushed down the dead man's throat.'

Warwick ceased. This last had been a long, unbroken recital, and mechanically he picked up his empty glass as if to drain it. The action brought me back to nearly normal. I rang for the waiter— the knob of the electric bell luckily being just over my head. While waiting, I had time to speak.

'I've heard enough,' I said hurriedly, 'to last me a lifetime. You've made me feel positively sick. But there's just one point. What happened to Macy? Did he live?'

Warwick nodded.

'That's another strange fact. He still lives. He was tried for the murder of Thring, but there was no real evidence. On the other hand, his story was too tall to be believed, with the result—well, you can guess.'

'A lunatic asylum—for life?' I asked.

Warwick nodded again. Then I followed his glance. A waiter was standing by my chair.

'Two double whisky-and-sodas,' I ordered tersely, and then, with shaking fingers, lighted a cigarette.

Mrs Raeburn's Waxwork

By Lady Eleanor Smith

The rain, which had poured with a pitiless ferocity for so long upon the chimneys and roofs of the great manufacturing city, seemed at length to enclose the whole town within towering prison-walls of burnished steel. It was now afternoon; the short winter day was nearly over, and it had rained thus from dawn, would probably continue to rain throughout the night. A dark, wet dusk began to envelop the city like a sable blanket; the street-lamps sprang into life, looming ahead like the ghosts of drowned and weary daffodils, casting watery and trembling reflections upon the shining rivers that were pavements. There were few people walking the mournful streets, and those that were had to struggle and batter their way through sharp gusts of wind, bent double beneath dripping and top-heavy umbrellas.

Such a one was Patrick Lamb, and so great was his hurry that more than once as he stumbled over an unperceived kerb he ran the risk of entangling both himself and his umbrella in the foaming, muddy torrents of the gutters beneath his feet. He had every reason to hurry; he was on his way to apply for a job, and he feared that unless he hastened he would be too late to secure this vacancy which meant so much to him.

Turning at last into a dark and narrow street, he saw opposite to him a ramshackle building of yellow brick, from the roof of which swelled forth a glass dome encrusted with the dirt and soot of ages. A flight of shallow steps led to a swing door. This was his destination.

He flung open the door and was immediately confronted by a turnstile, near which sat a seedy-looking man in an ill-fitting uniform not unlike that of a fireman.

'Sixpence, please,' said the man, and whistled through his teeth.

Patrick Lamb shook his head.

'No... I'm not a visitor. I have an appointment with Mr Mugivan, the manager.'

'Ah—ha,' said the attendant knowingly, and showed him into a tiny slice of a room filled with papers, files, account-books and dust. Here sat Mr Mugivan, a fat, podgy man with thick legs and a face like a tomato.

'Good afternoon,' said Patrick Lamb hesitatingly, 'I hear that you have a vacancy here for an—an attendant.'

Mr Mugivan stared for a moment at the young man's sallow, rather long face, at his deep-set grey eyes and slender, puny body.

'Who told you so?'

'My landlady, in Bury Street. She knew the last man you had here.'

'And what made you come?'

'Necessity. I'm in need of work. I was stranded here a week ago with a theatrical company'

There was a silence. Mr Mugivan suddenly laughed, looking at his visitor rather defiantly with little red-rimmed eyes that were not unlike the eyes of a pig.

'Rather a come-down, isn't it, for an actor to find himself minding Mugivan's Waxworks?'

'That doesn't matter—sir. And, if you'll only let me, I'll mind them damn well.'

'It's long hours,' said the proprietor, still speaking contemptuously. 'Nine in the morning till seven at night. An hour for lunch and an hour for tea. Two pounds a week—and the attendant has to wear a uniform. *An actor* wouldn't fancy that, would he?'

'Maybe I'm not an actor,' said Patrick Lamb.

Mr Mugivan spat upon the floor.

'I'll give you a trial, anyhow. What's your name?'

Patrick told him.

'Well, Lamb,' and the proprietor creaked himself out of his chair, revealing incidentally that he wore carpet slippers and had bunions, 'come with me and I'll show you Mugivan's Beauties before you go. You can start tomorrow morning.'

Obediently Patrick followed his new employer through the turnstile, which was swung round obligingly by the other attendant, down a narrow white-washed tunnel into a large apartment.

'Ever seen figures before?' inquired Mr Mugivan.

'Waxworks? Not since I was a kid.'

'Hall of Monarchs,' said Mr Mugivan, sucking his teeth with a deprecating sound.

The room in which they found themselves was bare and vault-like; here, too, the walls were white-washed; the floor was covered with a red drugget, and in the middle of the room was placed a sofa upholstered in shabby crimson plush. Yet although bare the room was not empty, but crowded, crowded with a pale throng of mute and stiff and silent figures. They stood in groups, a dais to each group, and were protected from the public by a red cord which imprisoned them, like sheep in a pen, so that had they wished they could not have strayed, but must for ever remain captive. There they stood and would no doubt stand throughout the ages, these tinsel kings and queens, Plantagenets and Stuarts, Tudors and Hanoverians, calm and blank and dreadfully remote, pallid of cheek and glassy of eye, indifferent to all who passed by to gape at them—a host of waxen princes, all dead, many of them forgotten, terribly isolated in their garish splendour, uncannily galvanized into a crude semblance of life that yet denied them even the elements of life, leaving them fixed, frozen and staring, while the dust thickened upon their cheap and fusty robes of purple and sham ermine.

Opposite the door through which they had come was another door leading to yet another chamber. Mr Mugivan led the way.

'Curiosities and Horrors,' he explained carelessly. They passed through the second door.

Here was another room, replica of the first, but more dimly lit, more melancholy than even the Hall of Monarchs, since the illumination that winked upon this dreary scene was greenish, ghastly, such a light as might have been expected to proceed from a sconce of corpse candles. Here were more massed ranks of still, impassive figures, paler these than the monarchs in the dim grotto of their melancholy chamber, and more repellent perhaps because their stiff, indifferent bodies were clothed in the garments of everyday and borrowed no majesty from princes' robes, however sham. A skeleton gleamed white in one corner of the room, there was a stuffed ox with six legs, a tiny waxen midget and a giant of local fame. Save for these the room was peopled only with men who had killed and who had paid the penalty for killing.

A throng staring before them, expressionless, rigid, mask-like, brooding perhaps upon their crimes.

Mr Mugivan seemed more at home in the second room. He became almost conversational.

'Here's Hopkins, the Norwich strangler... Tracey, who shot a policeman... John Joseph Gilmore, cut the throats of his wife and two children. . .'

They moved across the room. Then, near the slit of a window, crossed by iron bars, Patrick saw her for the first time. She stood on a little dais by herself, a young woman, or, rather, the effigy of a young woman, dressed neatly in dark clothes that were already old-fashioned in cut. She carried herself proudly, like a queen, and whereas the other waxworks were completely expressionless of countenance, this one alone, with proudly curling lips and short, imperious nose, seemed, he thought, actually to live, perhaps because she was disdain incarnate. She stood there easily, gracefully, long, pale hands folded upon her breast, and Patrick, gazing, felt the cool, amused stare of her grey eyes. For a moment his heart leaped sharply, startling him, and he had a sudden impulse to move forward and look more closely at her; then this sensation was succeeded by a creeping feeling of curious discomfort. He was embarrassed; he had to avert his eyes.

'Who's that woman?' he asked impetuously, and then wished that he had not spoken.

Mr Mugivan answered him casually, with his back turned to the effigy.

'That's Mrs Raeburn, the poisoner...and that's the lot, so come on.'

'Mrs Raeburn? I seem to know the name.'

'No doubt, no doubt. It was well enough known at one time.'

They walked away towards the Hall of Monarchs, and Patrick was acutely conscious of the supercilious grey eyes that must be gazing after them. The sham eyes of a sham woman, a waxen effigy! He felt acutely ridiculous.

Mr Mugivan said no more until they found themselves once again in the little office. Then, offering Patrick a cigarette, he asked suddenly, 'You're not a fanciful sort of chap by any chance?'

'Fanciful? You mean nervous? No, I can't say that I am. Why?'

'No place for fancies, this,' confided Mr Mugivan, waving his hand in the direction of the exhibition; 'it's a lonely sort of a job most of the time, and once you start thinking the figures are looking at you, well, you're done, that's all. Last chap we had here took to having fancies. That's why you've got his job.'

Patrick felt suddenly rebellious.

'I can safely say I shan't have fancies,' he said, laughing. 'I may not be particularly brave—in fact I'm not—but I must say it would take more than a parcel of wax dolls to scare me.'

'Figures aren't dolls,' Mr Mugivan corrected, shocked.

'Figures, then,' and he thought, 'Talking of figures, that woman Mrs Raeburn's got a good one.'

But neither he nor Mr Mugivan mentioned the name of the woman poisoner aloud.

'Nine o'clock tomorrow, then,' said Mr Mugivan.

'Nine o'clock tomorrow.'

And so they parted.

He discovered, the next day, two things about his new job. One was that his long and often lonely vigil with the waxworks gave him at times the curious and eerie sensation of being buried alive in a vault filled with the dead, the other that, with the morning, Mrs Raeburn, poisoner, had become once more a waxen effigy, and was no longer a living, breathing woman. This was comforting, yet in some strange way disappointing, for it was idle to deny that he had thought of her very frequently during the course of the night, and that the prospect of meeting once more the direct gaze of her rather mocking eyes had undoubtedly stimulated him and sent him forth into the cheerless streets kindled with an eager, sparkling excitement which he rather half-heartedly strove to suppress.

As the morning dragged by he studied a catalogue of the exhibition, trying to memorize the many dossiers of princes and murderers. He was accustomed to learn by heart, and in three hours his task was almost complete, yet with one exception. A curious revulsion prevented him from reading, even to himself, the brief account in the catalogue of Mrs Raeburn's crime, of discovering, through the medium of one cheap, smudged paragraph, that she had been an infamous woman, a monster of vice and cruelty. Taking a pen-knife from his pocket he cut away from his catalogue all record of her dark deeds. Yet she remained throughout the morning a lifeless effigy, and after glancing at her once, he gladly looked away.

He went out to lunch and returned for the long vigil of the afternoon. Few people came to visit the exhibition: a pair of school-children in charge of a maiden aunt, two girls, who giggled and eyed him coyly, an old man, and an amorous couple who plainly regarded his presence as a nuisance.

It was foggy outside; dusk fell early. For the first time that day, as he paced the Hall of Monarchs, he became sensible of the loneliness of his position. Once again the feeling of being buried among the dead returned to him, intensified this time by a bored and brooding melancholy, whereas in the morning there had also been a sense of apartment, smote lugubriously upon his ears. He would have liked to smoke, but this was, of course, forbidden.

At length he turned, and obeying an impulse which was becoming every second stronger, he moved towards the farther clumber, the Hall of Curiosities and Horrors. Here the twilight struck gloomily upon the wan and glimmering faces of the murderers, upturned to greet the first dark, smoky greyness of night: greenish they were once more, and dismal; and very hopeless in the blank resignation of their weary vigil in this dim room that was filled with the very breath of genteel decay.

He went straight towards the figure of Mrs Raeburn, standing tall and quiet and erect on her dais below the barred window. He had never been so near to her before; their eyes met, and once more she had recaptured that spark of life which had so curiously impressed him on the previous day. He gazed for some moments at her pale, clear-cut face, at her direct, ironic eyes. She appeared to return his scrutiny gravely, earnestly, scornfully, yet with a glint of interest and humour in her regard. She seemed, he thought, a woman well used to curious eyes, well able to defend herself against the stares of the inquisitive. Suddenly to his immense astonishment, he spoke to her, and his voice rang out strangely enough in that silent room.

'I wonder what you have done?' he asked her abruptly. 'For God's sake, what can you have done that you should be here?'

There was a long pause, during the course of which he continued to examine her closely. Was it his imagination, or did her lips really curve, was there an answering twinkle in her eye? And then he turned sharply, for he had caught, or thought that he had caught, a soft, eager rustling sound from the throng of effigies behind his back. And suddenly he was saved, for two little boys came pattering in to visit the curiosities and horrors.

The next day saw him resolutely keeping to the Hall of Monarchs. Here, with the lifeless dummies of long dead kings, he was safe. In that other room he realized that he was in peril. And the day after, although he hungered for a glimpse of Mrs Raeburn's pale face, he still remained aloof. The next day was Saturday, with a steady stream of patrons who would have made the dankest vault seem homely and prosaic. Then Sunday, a holiday.

On Monday he returned to the exhibition ready to laugh at himself for a morbid fool. The rain had stopped; a feeble ray of primrose sunshine, filtering through the barred window of the second chamber, made even Mrs Raeburn seem little more than a cunningly fashioned doll of life size. And he had spoken to her, as though she were alive and could hear and understand him! He was disgusted with himself.

Yet, with the swiftly flowing dusk the murderers changed once more; assumed as was their wont with the shades of night the vivid and evil personalities they must have worn during their life-time; seemed to stretch themselves as though released from some long spell of immobility; nodded, perhaps, to one another—even winked; perhaps brushed the dust from their shabby garments, smothered yawns, and waited, quietly expectant, for the closing of the exhibition. So Patrick thought, but it was difficult to see, for the shadows were thick in this lost and forgotten room.

He went towards the effigy of Mrs Raeburn and was not surprised to find that her eyes, alive and brilliant, almost feverish in their eager intensity, remained fixed direct upon him as though she waited to see whether he would, after his three days' absence, speak once more to her.

He was, however silent. He stared at her proud and beau-tiful mouth, at her long, pale hands, at the white stem of her throat, and admitted to himself that he desired her. 'Yet he had no immediate wish to touch her, but only longed passionately for the stiff, waxen body of this effigy to melt and transform itself into warm living flesh and blood. Somewhere, somehow, this miracle must be accomplished, for if he was unable to possess her he thought that, such was the spell she had cast upon him, he must inevitably pine and sicken, for she was La Belle Dame Sans Merci, and he was in her thrall. At last he spoke to her, softly, scarcely knowing that he spoke.

'You are a witch,' he said, 'and you possess me body and soul. You ought to be burnt, and since you are made of wax it should not be difficult to destroy you... I have a good mind to try.'

This time there was no mistake; a gleam of sardonic laughter came to her eyes, a strange and elfin smile to her curling lips. She defied him. And as before, the row of murderers behind seemed to move simultaneously with the rustling murmur of excitement. As before, too, he was saved by a footstep from the outer world. He turned sharply. A woman came into the room.

Patrick stiffened, became once more the respectful and vigilant attendant. The woman hesitated for a moment, then approached him slowly, for she was bent and squat and elderly, and walked with the help of a stick. He noticed vaguely that she was dressed in dingy black, with a frowsy bonnet askew upon her head and a film of veil that partially concealed her face. He bent down politely.

'Yes, madam? Is there anything I can do?'

'There is,' said the old woman. Her voice was clear and decisive, the voice of one who is accustomed to command. 'I have stupidly neglected to buy a catalogue at the door, and as I am old, and not so good a walker as I was, I wonder if you would save my going back by being kind enough to tell me something about the waxworks. These are murderers, are they not?'

Patrick, only too pleased to occupy his mind in this accustomed fashion, began mechanically:

'Yes, madam. There on my right is Richard Sayers, the Scottish body-snatcher, who shot two men before he was arrested, and protested his innocence to the last... Next to Sayers is Mugivan's conception of Jack the Ripper, the criminal who was never capcaptured...this figure is modelled according to the description of his appearance given to the police by those persons who protested that they had seen him before or after his appalling crimes... Next to Jack the Ripper we have Landru...'

But while his voice droned on he was dreading the moment when they must face Mrs Raeburn, when he would look once more upon her pale, remote face and meet once again her steady, contemptuous gaze. He lingered beside the midget, the freakish ox, the local giant. The old woman listened to him attentively, beady eyes darting from beneath her heavy veil. Once or twice she asked him a question, but otherwise was silent, seeming pleasantly absorbed in his monotonous catalogue of grim and fiendish crimes. At last the moment dreaded by Patrick could be postponed no longer; at last they faced the figure of Mrs Raeburn, standing slim and straight and self-possessed beneath the grating window. Suddenly Patrick remembered that he knew nothing of this murderess save that she had killed by poison; here he was speechless and could recite no bloodthirsty dossier, nor did he even know her victim; only that she was young and fair and that she had cast a spell upon him, and these things could not be told to his companion. There was a pause during the course of which the old woman examined the wax figure attentively and in silence. A length he mumbled:

'This is Mrs Raeburn...the poisoner.'

As he spoke he shot a sharp glance at the effigy and observed that she was blank and mask-like once more; indifferent both to him and his companion. His witch had again become a waxwork.

The old lady shuffled closer to the figure, peered with a certain attentive inquisitiveness, then turned to him and remarked critically.

'The likeness is not very good.'

He was startled, and gaped, unable quite to grasp the purport of her words.

He asked: 'You knew her?'

She did not answer him, but said, still peering: 'She was taller, she had more dignity, more of an air. And I think she was wilder. But it's long ago,' and her face changed all the time.

He asked again, trembling, his hands clammy cold, his voice unconsciously menacing: 'You knew her?'

For the first time the old creature turned to look at him, seeming to observe him closely. She chuckled, and at first he thought that one of the waxworks had laughed, so ghostly, so unexpected, was this little bubbling sound in the quietness of the dim hall.

She said, still chuckling: 'I am Mrs Raeburn.'

And as he did not answer she pulled back her veil. She was younger than he had at first supposed. She revealed a fat, gross, heavy-jowled face, sallow, unhealthy, with high Mongolian cheekbones. Her nose was squat and thick, her cheeks carved with two deep-cut lines running from her nostrils to the corners of her mouth. Her little sharp grey eyes were almost buried in folds of flesh. Beneath the shoddy bonnet a strand of hair hung untidily; it was dyed a bright orange tint. The face, which leered forth so boldly at Patrick, was seamed and stamped with the marks of every foul and obscene vice; brazen, debauched, so brutal as to be three parts animal, it seemed to hang in the air, this gargoyle face, to gloat triumphantly upon his horror and confusion. Then, swiftly, the woman whisked back her veil and said crisply in her clear and resonant voice:

'It didn't do me justice, your image.' Then in a moment she was gone, while behind her the effigy of Mrs Raeburn, poisoner, remained standing cool and pale and remote upon her dais, all the paler, all the cooler, for being now the centre of a flood of cold and frozen moonlight.

Patrick fled after the old woman, not because he wished to see her again, but because of the two of them the waxen image had become the more repulsive, yet, when he reached the Hall of Monarchs, she had already disappeared.

He waited, sick and shivering, until the clock struck seven and the show shut down, then he went in search of Mr Mugivan, whom he found in his office, reading an evening paper, with his feet on his desk.

'Good evening,' said Patrick. 'I want to tell you something.'

Mr Mugivan put down his paper.

'My word, young fellow, you look cheap. What is it now?'

Patrick, gulping, said: 'Do you know who's been here this afternoon?'

'I do not,' said Mr Mugivan. 'I'm proprietor of a waxwork show, not a magician. Who has been here?'

'Mrs Raeburn. The real Mrs Raeburn. She came to see her waxwork. She's just gone.'

As Mr Mugivan gaped, his red face became curiously mottled—white and purple in patches, Patrick noticed dispassionately.

'Mrs Raeburn?'

'Yes.'

Mr Mugivan climbed laboriously from his chair.

'Mrs Raeburn, eh? Somebody's been pulling your leg. You don't know your catalogue, either. Mrs Raeburn indeed?'

And he pulled a document from the untidy desk, licked his thumb, and flipped over a page.

'Mrs Raeburn,' he said, speaking very loud and not looking at Patrick, 'was scragged—hanged, you understand—hanged by the neck for the murder of her husband more than twenty years ago. That being so, you could hardly have seen her here just now. And that's enough of your funny stuff for one day.'

Patrick said nothing. There was really nothing to say. Nor did Mr Mugivan break the silence, but waddled to and fro about the little room, changing his carpet slippers for boots, struggling into his overcoat, cramming a check cap upon his head. In a moment he had gone.

Patrick switched off the office light, then went forth, as was his custom, to extinguish the gas jets in the exhibition before locking up for the night. His comrade of the turnstile had already gone home; he was alone, entirely alone, with more than a hundred waxen effigies. It was now quite dark outside, for the moon had fled behind a screen of clouds, and there was a rushing sound of strong wind, which swept in gusts past the shuttered windows.

He paused to light a forbidden cigarette, and then it was that he realized with an odd detachment that what he had seen during the afternoon was not a ghost, but something even more monstrous—a disembodied soul. The foul and evil soul of this wretched woman whose lovely image had bewitched him. The hideous reflection of a hideous mind. Behind her seeming purity and beauty had always been this horror, dormant, waiting to leap forth and devour. The wind rose, moaning, battering at the panes.

On such a night, he mused, as he tramped towards the monarchs, ghouls would surely stalk abroad and witches soar through the air clutching their broomsticks and screaming aloud their lust for Satan. Vampires, sorcerers, fiends. A nightmare pack of horrors... He stretched on tip-toe to lower the gas above the wan, impassive face of King Richard II... And in the old days witches were burnt alive like the guys now consumed by flames each Fifth of November... And after burning he supposed that these evil women could do no more harm, but were destroyed for ever, they and their spells. A good job, too. He entered the second chamber.

☒

That night the inhabitants of the city were surprised to perceive a crimson flush sweeping the sky above the roof-tops of a distant street. Then came a clanging of bells, a roar of motor-engines, and, hot-foot, in pursuit of the fire brigade, a yelling, excited rabble. Mugivan's Waxwork Exhibition was on fire. No one wanted to miss the show, doubly welcome because it was free.

The wind was strong that night, and licked the flames eagerly, strengthening them until the efforts of the men armed with hose-pipes became pathetic in their futility. At length the roof crashed in, and a wall of roaring flame rose as though to leap into the sky. They were triumphant, these pillars of fire, as though they knew that they were purifying, destroying a witch.

By morning Mugivan's Waxwork Show was a drenched and sooty ruin. Many of the figures were entirely destroyed, the monarchs having been on the whole unluckier than the murderers. Down in the Hall of Curiosities and Horrors there were a few survivors. Some were quite intouched. Mrs Raeburn, for instance, appeared to have emerged unscathed from the ordeal, and stood upon her dais proudly and gracefully, pale hands folded demurely upon her breast. And yet, on closer inspection, Mrs Raeburn proved not to be entirely unharmed. Her waxen face had melted, and running, the stuff had twisted upon her features a strange and devilish sneer. Save for her pride of carriage she was unrecognizable, distorted. And then the firemen made a further discovery.

Lying nearby, where the flames had crackled most fiercely, was charred and sodden bundle of dothing. They bent to examine it. It was, they found, a human body, the body of a young man.

A Face in the Night

By Ruskin Bond

It may give you some idea of rural humour if I begin this tale with an anecdote that concerns me. I was walking alone through a village at night when I met an old man carrying a lantern. I found, to my surprise, that the man was blind.

'Old man,' I asked, 'if you cannot see, why do you carry a lamp?'

'I carry this,' he replied, 'so that fools do not stumble against me in the dark.'

This incident has only a slight connection with the story that follows, but I think it provides the right sort of tone and setting. Mr Oliver, an Anglo-Indian teacher, was returning to his school late one night, on the outskirts of the hill station of Simla. The school was conducted on English public school lines and the boys, most of them from well-to- do Indian families, wore blazers, caps, and ties. *Life* magazine's a feature on India had once called this school the "Eton of the East".

Individuality was not encouraged; they were all destined to become 'leaders of men'.

Mr Oliver had been teaching in the school for several years. Sometimes it seemed like an eternity; for one day followed upon another with the same monotonous routine. The Simla bazaar, with its cinemas and restaurants, was about two miles from the school; and Mr Oliver, a bachelor, usually strolled into the town in the evening returning after dark, when he would take a short cut through a pint forest.

When there was a strong wind, the pine trees made sad, eerie sounds that kept most people to the main road. But Mr Oliver was not a nervous or imaginative man. He carried a torch and, on the night I write of, its pale gleam—the batteries were running down—moved fitfully over the narrow forest path. When its flickering light fell on the figure of a boy who was sitting alone on a rock, Mr Oliver stopped. Boys were not supposed to be out of school after 7 p.m., and it was now well past nine.

'What are you doing out here, boy?' asked Mr Oliver sharply, moving closer so that he could recognize the miscreant. But even as he approached the boy, Mr Oliver sensed that something was wrong. The boy appeared to be crying. His head hung down, he held his face in his hands, and his body shook convulsively. It was a strange, soundless weeping, and Mr Oliver felt distinctly uneasy.

'Well—what's the matter?' he asked, his anger giving way to concern. 'What are you crying for?' The boy would not answer or look up. His body continued to be racked with silent sobbing.

'Come on, boy, you shouldn't be out here at this hour. Tell me the trouble. Look up!'

The boy looked up. He took his hands from his face and looked up at his teacher. The light from Mr Oliver's torch fell on the boy's face—if you could call it a face.

He had no eyes, ears, nose, or mouth. It was just a round smooth head—with a school cap on top of it. And that's where the story should end—as indeed it has for several people who have had similar experiences and dropped dead of inexplicable heart attacks. But for Mr Oliver it did not end there.

The torch fell from his trembling hand. He turned and scrambled down the path, running blindly through the trees and calling for help. He was still running towards the school buildings when he saw a lantern swinging in the middle of the path. Mr Oliver had never before been so pleased to see the night-watchman. He stumbled up to the watchman, gasping for breath and speaking incoherently.

'What is it, Sir?' asked the watchman. 'Has there been an accident? Why are you running?'

'I saw something—something horrible—a boy weeping in the forest—and he had no face!'

'No face, Sir?'

'No eyes, nose, mouth—nothing.'

'Do you mean it was like this, Sir?' asked the watchman, and raised the lamp to his own face. The watchman had no eyes, no ears, no features at all—not even an eyebrow!

The wind blew the lamp out, and Mr Oliver had his heart attack.

Henry

By Phyllis Bottome

For four hours every morning and for twenty minutes before a large audience at night Fletcher was locked up with murder. It glared at him from twelve pairs of amber eyes; it clawed the air close to him, it spat naked hate at him, and watched with uninterrupted intensity to catch him for one moment off his guard.

Fletcher had only his will and his eyes to keep death at bay.

Of course, outside the cage into which Fletcher shut himself nightly with his twelve tigers were the keepers, standing at intervals around it with concealed pistols; but they were outside it. The idea was that if anything happened to Fletcher they would be able by prompt action to get him out alive; but they had his private instructions to do nothing of the kind, to shoot straight at his heart, and pick off the guilty tiger afterwards to cover their intention. Fletcher knew better than to try to preserve anything the tigers left of him, if once they had started in.

The lion-tamer in the next cage was better off than Fletcher, he was intoxicated by a rowdy vanity which dimmed fear. He stripped himself half naked every night, covered himself with ribbons, and thought so much of himself that he hardly noticed his lions. Besides, his lions had all been born in captivity, were slightly doped, and were only lions.

Fletcher's tigers weren't doped because dope dulled their fears of the whip and didn't dull their ferocity; captivity softened nothing in them, and they hated man.

Fletcher had taught tigers since he was a child; his father had started him on baby tigers, who were charming. They hurt you as much as they could with an absent-minded roguishness difficult to resist; what was death to you was play to them; but as they couldn't kill him, all the baby a loud, contented, pleasant noise. Henry was purring!

Fletcher's voice changed from the sharp brief order like the crack if a whip into a persuasive companionable drawl. Henry's eyes reopened; he rose, stood rigid for a moment, and then slowly the rigidity melted out of his powerful form. Once more that answering look came into the tiger's eyes. He stared straight at Fletcher without blinking and jumped on his tub. He sat on it impassively, his tail waving, his great jaws closed. He eyed Fletcher attentively and without hate. Then Fletcher knew that this tiger was not as other tigers, not as any other tiger.

He threw down his whip, Henry never moved; he approached Henry, lifted his lip to snarl, thought better of it, and permitted the approach. Fletcher took his life in his hand and touched Henry.

Henry snarled mildly, but his great claws remained closed; his eyes expressed nothing but a gentle warning; they simply said: 'You know, I don't like being touched; be careful, I might have to claw you!' Fletcher gave a brief nod; he knew the margin of safety was slight but he had a margin. He could do something with Henry.

Hour after hour everyday he taught Henry; but he taught him without a pistol or whip. It was unnecessary to use anything beyond his voice and his eyes. Henry read his eyes eagerly. When he failed to catch Fletcher's meaning, Fletcher's voice helped him out. Henry did not always understand even Fletcher's voice, but where he differed from the other tigers was that he wished to understand; nor had he from the first the slightest inclination to kill Fletcher.

He used to sit for hours at the back of his cage waiting for Fletcher. When he heard far off—unbelievably far off—the sound of Fletcher's step, he moved forward to the front of his cage and prowled restlessly to and fro till Fletcher unlocked the door and entered. Then Henry would crouch back a little, politely, from no desire to avoid his friend, but as a mere tribute to the superior power he felt in Fletcher. Directly Fletcher spoke, he came forward proudly and exchanged their wordless eye language.

Henry liked doing his tricks alone with Fletcher. He jumped on and off his tub following the mere wave of Fletcher's hand. He soon went further, jumped on a high stool and leapt through a large white paper disc held up by Fletcher. Although the disc looked as if he couldn't possibly get through it, yet the clean white sheet always yielded to his impact; he did get through it, blinking a little, but feeling a curious pride that he had faced the odious thing—and pleased Fletcher.

He let Fletcher sit on his back, though the mere touch of an alien creature was repulsive to him. But he stood perfectly still, his hair rising a little, his teeth bared, a growl half suffocated in his throat. He told himself it was Fletcher. He must control his impulse to fling him off and tear him up.

In all the rehearsals and performances in the huge arena, full of strange noises, blocked with alien human beings, Henry led the other tigers; and though Fletcher's influence over him was weakened, he still recognized it. Fletcher seemed farther away from him at these times, less sympathetic and godlike, but Henry tried hard to follow the intense persuasive eyes and the brief emphatic voice; he would not lose touch even with this attenuated ghost of Fletcher.

It was with Henry and Henry alone that Fletcher dared his nightly stunt, dropped the whip and stick at his feet and let Henry do his tricks as he did them in his cage alone, with nothing beyond Fletcher's eyes and voice to control him. The other eleven tigers, beaten, glaring and snarling on to their tubs, sat impassively despising Henry's unnatural docility. He had the chance they had always wanted, and he didn't take it—what kind of tiger was he?

But Henry ignored the other tigers. Reluctantly standing with all four feet together on his tub, he contemplated a further triumph. Fletcher stood before him, holding a stick between his hands and above his head, intimately, compellingly through the language of his eyes Fletcher told Henry to jump from his tub over his head. What Fletcher said was: 'Come on, old thing! Jump! Come on! I'll duck in time. You won't hurt me! It's my stunt! Stretch your old paws together and jump!'

And Henry jumped. He hated the dazzling lights, loathed the hard, unexpected, senseless sounds which followed his leap, and he was secretly terrified that he would land on Fletcher. But it was very satisfactory when, after his rush through the air, he found he hadn't touched Fletcher, but had landed on another tub carefully prepared for him; and Fletcher said to him as plainly as possible before he did the drawer trick with the other tigers: 'Well! You are a one-er, and no mistake!'

The drawer trick was the worst of Fletcher's stunts. He had to put a table in the middle of the cage and whip each tiger up to it. When he had them placed each on his tub around the table he had to feed them with a piece of raw meat deftly thrown at the exact angle to reach the special tiger for which it was intended, and to avoid contract with eleven other tigers ripe to dispute his intention. Fletcher couldn't afford the slightest mistake or a fraction of delay.

Each tiger had to have in turn his piece of raw meat, and the drawer shut after it—opened—the next morsel thrown exactly into the grasp of the next tiger, and so on until the twelve were fed.

Fletcher always placed Henry at his back. Henry snatched in turn his piece of raw meat, but he made no attempt, as the other tigers always did, to take anyone else's; and Fletcher felt the safer for knowing that Henry was at his back. He counted on Henry's power to protect him more than he counted on the four keepers standing outside the cage with their pistols. More than once, when one of the other tigers turned restive, Fletcher had found Henry rigid, but very light on his toes, close to his side, between him and danger.

The circus manager spoke to Fletcher warningly about his foolish infatuation for Henry.

'Mark my words, Fletcher,' he said, 'the tiger doesn't live that wouldn't do you in if it could. You give Henry too many chances—one day he'll take one of them.' But Fletcher only laughed. He knew

Henry, he had seen the soul of the great tiger leap to his eyes and shine there in answer to his own eyes. A man does not kill his god; at least not willingly. It is said that two thousand years ago he did some such thing, through ignorance, but Fletcher forgot this incident. Besides, on the whole, he believed more in Henry than he did in his fellow-men.

This was not surprising, because Fletcher had very little time for human fellowship. When he was not teaching tigers not to kill him, he rested from the exhaustion of the nerves which comes from a prolonged companionship with eager, potential murders; and the rest of the time Fletcher boasted of Henry to the lion-tamer, and taught Henry new tricks.

Macormack, the lion-tamer, had a very good stunt lion, and he was extravagantly jealous of Henry. He could not make his lion go out backwards before him from the arena cage into the passage as Henry had learned to do before Fletcher, and when he had tried Ajax had, not seriously, but with an intention rather more than playful, flung him against the bars of the cage.

Macormack brooded deeply on this slight from his pet, and determined to take it out of Fletcher's.

'Pooh!' he said. 'You call yourself damned plucky for laying your ole 'oof on 'Enry's scruff, and e' don't calf look wicked while you're doin' it. Why don't ye put yer cead in 'is mouf and be done with it? That cud be talking, that would!'

'I wouldn't mind doing it,' said Fletcher reflectively, after a brief pause, 'once I get him used to the idea. 'Is jaw aint so big as a lion's, still I could get the top of me 'ead in.'

The lion-tamer swaggered off jeering, and Fletcher thought out how best to lay this new trick before Henry for his approval.

But from the first Henry didn't approve of it. He showed quite plainly that he didn't want his head touched. He didn't like his mouth held forcibly open, and wouldn't have anything put between his teeth without crunching. Fletcher wasted several loaves of bread over the effort—and only succeeded once or twice gingerly and very ungracefully in getting portions of his own head in and out in safety. Henry roared long and loudly at him, clawed the air, and flashed all the language he could from his flaming eyes into Fletcher's, to explain that this thing wasn't done between tigers! It was hitting below the belt! An infringement of an instinct too deep for him to master: and Fletcher knew that he was outraging Henry's instinct, and decided to refrain.

'It ain't fair to my tiger!' he said to himself regretfully; and he soothed Henry with raw meat and endearments, promising to refrain from his unnatural venture.

But when the hour for the performance came, Fletcher forgot his promise. He was enraged at Macormack's stunt lion for getting more than his share of the applause. He had the middle cage, and what with the way Macormack swaggered half naked in his scarlet ribbons, and the lion roared—the pulverising, deep-toned, desert roar—and yet did all his tricks one after the other like a little gentleman, it did seem as if Henry barely got a round of his due applause.

Henry jumped through his white disc—so did the stunt lion! He took his leap over Fletcher's head—the stunt lion did something flashy with a drum, not half as dangerous, and the blind and ignorant populace ignored Henry and preferred the drum.

'I don't care!' said Fletcher to himself, 'Henry's got to take my head in his mouth whether he likes it or not—that'll starde 'em!'

He got rid of all the other tigers. Henry was used to that, he liked it; now he would do his own final stunt—walk out backwards into the passage which led to the cages, and Fletcher would hurry out through the arena and back to Henry's cage, give him a light extra supper, and tell him what a fine tiger he was.

But Fletcher called him into the middle of the state instead and made him take that terrible attitude he had taught him for the new trick. His eyes said: 'You'll do this once for me, old man, won't you?'

Henry's eyes said: 'Don't ask it! I'm tired! I'm hungry! I want to get out!'

But Fletcher wouldn't read Henry's eyes anymore. He tried to force his head sideways into the terrible open jaws, and Henry's teeth, instinctive, reluctant, compelled, closed on Fletcher's neck.

What Henry minded after the momentary relief of his instinctive action was the awful stillness of Fletcher. It wasn't the stillness of the arena—that was nothing, a mere deep indrawn breath. Fletcher lay limp between his paws, as if the trick were over, as if all tricks were over. He wouldn't get up, he didn't look at Henry. Henry's eyes gazed down unblinkingly into the blank eyes of Fletcher. All Henry's soul was in his eyes, watching for Fletcher's soul to rise to meet them. And for an age nothing happened, until at last Henry realized that nothing ever would.

Before the nearest keeper shot Henry, Henry knew that he had killed his god. He lifted up his heavy painted head and roared out through the still arena, a loud despairing cry.

His heart was pierced before they reached his heart.

The Interloper

By Saki (H.H. Munro)

In a forest of mixed growth somewhere on the eastern spurs of the Carpathians, a man stood one winter night watching and listening, as though he waited for some beast of the woods to come within the range of his vision, and, later, of his rifle. But the game for whose presence he kept so keen an outlook was none that figured in the sportsman's calendar as lawful and proper for the chase. Ulrich von Gradwitz patrolled the dark forest in quest of a human enemy.

The forest lands of Gradwitz were of wide extent and well stocked with game, the narrow strip of precipitous woodland that lay on its outskirt was not remarkable for the game it harboured or the shooting it afforded, but it was the most jealously guarded of all its owner's territorial possessions. A famous lawsuit, in the days of his grandfather, had wrested it from the illegal possession of a neighbouring family of petty landowners, the dispossessed party had never acquiesced in the judgment of the Courts, and along series of poaching affrays and similar scandals had embittered the relationships between the families for three generations. The neighbour feud had grown into a personal one since Ulrich had come to be head of his family; if there was a man in the world whom he detested and wished ill to it was Georg Znaeym, the inheritor of the quarrel and the tireless game-snatcher and raider of the disputed border-forest. The feud might, perhaps, have died down or been compromised if the personal ill-will of the two men had not stood in the way; as boys they had thirsted for one another's blood, as men each prayed that misfortune might fall on the other, and this wind-scourged winter night Ulrich had banded together his foresters to watch the dark forest, not in quest of four-footed quarry, but to keep a lookout for the prowling thieves whom he suspected of being afoot from across the land boundary. The roebuck, which usually kept in the sheltered hollows during a storm-wind, were running like driven things tonight, and there was movement and unrest among the creatures that were wont to sleep through the dark hours. Assuredly there was a disturbing element in the forest, and Ulrich could guess the quarter from whence it came.

He strayed away by himself from the watchers whom he had placed in ambush on the crest of the hill, and wandered far down the steep slopes amid the wild tangle of undergrowth, peering through the tree trunks and listening through the whistling and skirling of the wind and the restless beating of the branches for sight or sound of the marauders. If only on this wild night, in this dark, lone spot, he might come across Georg Znaeym, man to man, with none to witness—that vas the wish that was uppermost in his thoughts. And as he stepped round the trunk of a huge beech he came face to face with the man he sought.

The two enemies stood glaring at one another for a long silent moment. Each had a rifle in his hand, each had hate in his heart and murder uppermost in his mind. The chance had come to give full play in the passions of a lifetime. But a man who has been brought up under the code of a restraining civilization cannot easily nerve himself to shoot down his neighbour in cold blood and without word spoken, except for an offence against his hearth and honour. And before the moment of hesitation had given way to action a deed of Nature's own violence overwhelmed them both. A fierce shriek of the storm had been answered by a splitting crash over their heads, and ere they could leap aside a mass of falling beech tree had thundered down on them. Ulrich von Gradwitz found himself stretched on the ground, one arm numb beneath him and the other held almost as helplessly in a tight tangle of forked branches, while both legs were pinned beneath the fallen mass. His heavy shooting-boots had saved his feet from being crushed to pieces, but if his fractures were not as serious as they might have been, at least it was evident that he could not move from his present position till someone came to release him. The descending twigs had slashed the skin of his face, and he had to wink away some drops of blood from his eyelashes before he could take in a general view of the disaster. At his side, so near that under ordinary circumstances he could almost have touched him, lay Georg Znaeym, alive and struggling, but obviously as helplessly pinioned down as himself. All round them lay a thick-strewn wreckage of splintered branches and broken twigs.

Relief at being alive and exasperation at his captive plight brought a strange medley of pious thank-offerings and sharp curses to Ulrich's lips. Georg, who was nearly blinded with the blood which trickled across his eyes, stopped his struggling for a moment to listen, and then gave a short, snarling laugh.

'So you're not killed, as you ought to be, but you're caught, anyway,' he cried, 'caught fast. Ho, what a jest. Ulrich von Gradwitz snared in his stolen forest. There's real justice for you!'

And he laughed again, mockingly and savagely, 'I'm caught in my own forest-land,' retorted Ulrich. 'When my men, come to release us you will wish, perhaps, that you were in a better plight than caught poaching on a neighbour's land, shame on you.' Georg was silent for a moment, then he answered quietly.

'Are you sure that your men will find much to release? I have men, too, in the forest tonight, close behind me, and *they* will be here first and do the releasing. When they drag me out from under these damned branches it won't need much clumsiness on their part to roll this mass of trunk right over on the top of you. Your men will find you dead under a fallen beech tree. For form's sake I shall send my condolences to your family'

'It is a useful hint,' said Ulrich fiercely 'My men had orders to follow in ten minutes' time, seven of which must have gone by already, and when they get me out—I will remember the hint. Only as you will have met your death poaching on my lands I don't think I can decently send any message of condolence to your family.'

'Good,' snarled Georg, 'good. We fight this quarrel out to the death, you and I and our foresters, with no cursed interlopers to come between us. Death and damnation to you, Ulrich von Grad-witz. 'The same to you, Georg Znaeym, forest thief, game-snatcher.' Both men spoke with the bitterness of possible defeat before them, for each knew that it might be long before his men would seek him out or find him; it was a bare matter of chance which party would arrive first on the scene.

Both had now given up the useless struggle to free themselves from the mass of wood that held them down; Ulrich limited his endeavours to an effort to bring his one partially free arm near enough to his outer coat-pocket to draw out his wine-flask. Even when he had accomplished that operation it was long before he could manage the unscrewing of the stopper or get any of the liquid down his throat. But what a Heaven-sent draught it seemed! It was an open winter, and little snow had fallen as yet, hence the captives suffered less from the cold than might have been the case at that season of the year; nevertheless, the wine was warming and reviving to the wounded man, and he looked across with something like a throb of pity to where his enemy lay, keeping the groans of pain and weariness from crossing his lips.

'Could you reach this flask if I threw it over to you?' asked Ulrich suddenly: 'there is good wine in it, and one may as well be as comfortable as one can. Let us drink, even if tonight one of us dies.'

'No, I can scarcely see anything, there is so much blood caked round my eyes,' said Georg, 'and in any case I don't drink wine with an enemy.'

Ulrich was silent for a few minutes, and lay listening to the weary screeching of the wind. An idea was slowly forming and growing in his brain, an idea that gained strength every time that he looked across at the man who was fighting so grimly against pain and exhaustion. In the pain and languor that Ulrich himself was feeling the old fierce hatred seemed to be dying down.

'Neighbour,' he said presently, 'do as you please if your men come first. It was a fair compact. But as for me, I've changed my mind. If my men are the first to come you shall be the first to be helped, as though you were my guest. We have quarrelled like devils all our lives over this stupid strip of forest, where the trees can't even stand upright in a breath of wind. Lying here tonight, thinking. I've come to think we've been rather fools; there are better things in life than getting the better of a boundary dispute. Neighbour, if you will help me to bury the old quarrel I—I will ask you to be my friend.'

Georg Znaeym was silent for so long that Ulrich thought, perhaps, he had fainted with the pain of his injuries. Then he spoke slowly and in jerks.

'How the whole region would stare and gabble if we rode into the market-square together. No one living can remember seeing a Znaeym and a von Gradwitz talking to one another in friendship. And what peace there would be among the forester folk if we ended our feud tonight. And if we choose to make peace among our people there is none other to interfere, no interlopers from outside... You would come and keep the Sylvester night beneath my roof, and I would come and feast on some high day at your castle... I would never fire a shot on your land, save when you invited me as a guest; and you should come and shoot with me down in the marshes where the wildfowl are. In all the countryside there are none that could hinder if we willed to make peace. I never thought to have wanted to do other than hate you all my life, but I think I have changed my mind about things too, this last half-hour. And you offered me your wine-flask... Ulrich von Gradwitz, I will be your friend '

For a space both men were silent, turning over in their minds the wonderful changes that this dramatic reconciliation would bring about. In the cold, gloomy forest, with the wind tearing in fitful gusts through the naked branches and whistling round the tree-trunks, they lay and waited for the help that would now bring release and succour to both parties. And each prayed a private prayer that his men might be the first to arrive, so that he might be the first to show honourable attention to the enemy that had become a friend.

Presently, as the wind dropped for a moment, Ulrich broke silence.

'Let's shout for help,' he said; 'in this lull our voices may carry a little way.'

'They won't carry far through the trees and undergrowth' said Georg, 'but we can try. Together then.'

The two raised their voices in a prolonged hunting call.

'Together again,' said Ulrich a few minutes later, after listening in vain for an answering halloo.

'I heard something that time, I think, said Ulrich.

'I heard nothing but the pestilential wind,' said Georg hoarsely.

There was silence again for some minutes, and then Ulrich gave a joyful cry.

'I can see figures coming through the wood. They are following in the way I came down the hillside.'

Both men raised their voices in as loud a shout as they could muster.

'They hear us! They've stopped. Now they see us. They're running down the hill towards us,' cried Ulrich.

'How many of them are there?' asked Georg.

'I can't see distinctly,' said Ulrich; 'nine or ten.'

'Then they are yours,' said Georg; 'I had only seven out with me.'

'They are making all the speed they can, brave lads,' said Ulrich gladly.

'Are they your men?' asked Georg. 'Are they your men?' he repeated impatiently as Ulrich did not answer.

'No,' said Ulrich with a laugh, the idiotic chattering laugh of a man unstrung with hideous fear.

'Who are they?' asked Georg quickly, straining his eyes to see what the other would gladly not have seen.

'*Wolves.*'

The Story of Medhans Lea

By E. and H. Heron

The following story has been put together from the account of the affair given by Nare-Jones, sometime house-surgeon at Bart's, of his strange terror and experiences both in Medhans Lea and the pallid avenue between the beeches; of the narrative of Savelsan, of what he saw and heard in the billiard room and afterwards; of the silent and indisputable witness of big, bullnecked Harland himself; and, lastly of the conversation which subsequently took place between these three men and Mr Flaxman Low, the noted psychologist.

It was by the merest chance that Harland and his two guests spent that memorable evening of 18 January 1899, in the house of Medhans Lea. The house stands on the slope of a partially-wooded ridge in one of the Midland Counties. It faces south, and overlooks a wide valley bounded by the blue outlines of the Bredon hills. The place is secluded, the nearest dwelling being a small public house at the crossroads some mile and a half from the lodge gates.

Medhans Lea is famous for its long straight avenue of beeches, and for other things. Harland, when he signed the lease, was thinking of the avenue of beeches; not of the other things, of which he knew nothing till later.

Harland had made his money by running tea plantations in Assam, and he owned all the virtues and faults of a man who has spent most of his life abroad. The first time he visited the house he weighed seventeen stone and ended most of his sentences with 'don't you know?' His ideas could hardly be said to travel on the higher planes of thought, and his chief aim in life was to keep himself down to die seventeen stone. He had a red neck and a blue eye, and was a muscular, inoffensive, good-natured man, with courage to spare, and an excellent voice for accompanying the banjo.

After singing the lease, he found that Medhans Lea needed an immense amount of putting in order and decorating. While this was being done, he came backwards and forwards to the nearest provincial town, where he stopped at a hotel, driving out almost daily to superintend the arrangements of his new habitation. Thus he had been away for the Christmas and New Year, but about 15 January he returned to the Red Lion, accompanied by his friends Nare-Jones and Savelsan, who proposed to move with him into his new house during the course of the ensuing week.

The immediate cause of their visit to Medhans Lea on the evening of the 18th was the fact that the billiard table at the Red Lion was not fit, as Harland remarked, to play shinty on, while there was an excellent table just put in at Medhans Lea, where the big billiard room in the left wing had a wide window with a view down a portion of the beech avenue.

'Hang it!' said Harland, 'I wish they would hurry up with the house. The painters aren't out of it yet, and the people don't come to the Lodge till Monday.'

'It's a pity, too,' remarked Savelsan regretfully, 'when you think of that table.'

Savelsan was an enthusiast in billiards, who spent all the time he could spare from his business, which happened to be teabroking, at the game. He was the more sorry for the delay, since Harland was one of the few men he knew to whom it was not necessary to give points.

'It's a ripping table,' returned Harland. 'Tell you what,' he added, struck by a happy idea, 'I'll send out Thomas to make tilings straight for us tomorrow, and we'll put a case of syphons and a bottle of whisky under the seat of the trap, and drive over for a game after dinner.'

The other two agreed to this arrangement, but in the morning Nare-Jones found himself obliged to run up to London to see about securing a berdi as ship's doctor. It was settled, however, that on his return he was to follow Harland and Savelsan to Medhans Lea.

He got back by the 8.30, entirely delighted, because he had booked a steamer bound for the Persian Gulf and Karachi, and had gained the cheering intelligence that a virulent type of cholera was lying in wait for the advent of the Mecca pilgrims in at any rate two of the chief ports of call, which would give him precisely the experience he desired.

Having dined, and the night being fine, he ordered a dogcart to take him out to Medhans Lea. The moon had just risen by the time he reached the entrance to the avenue, and as he was beginning to feel cold he pulled up, intending to walk to the house. Then he dismissed the boy and cart, a carriage having been ordered to come for the whole party after midnight. Nare-Jones stopped to light a cigar before entering the avenue, then he walked past the empty lodge. He moved briskly in the best possible temper with himself and all the world. The night was still, and his collar up, his feet fell silently on the dry carriage road, while his mind was away on blue water forecasting his voyage on the *S.S. Sumatra.*

He says he was quite halfway up the avenue before he became conscious of anything unusual. Looking up at the sky, he noticed what a bright, clear night it was, and how sharply defined the outline of the beeches stood out against the vault of heaven. The moon was yet low, and threw netted shadows of bare twigs and branches on the road which ran between black lines of trees in an almost straight vista up to the dead grey face of the house now barely two hundred yards away. Altogether it struck him as forming a pallid picture, etched in like a steel engraving in black, and grey, and white.

He was thinking of this when he was aware of words spoken rapidly in his ear, and he turned half expecting to see someone behind him. No one was visible. He had not caught the words, nor could he define the voice; but a vague conviction of some horrible meaning fixed itself in his consciousness.

The night was very still, ahead of him the house glimmered grey and shuttered in the moonlight. He shook himself, and walked on oppressed by a novel sensation compounded of disgust and childish fear; and still, from behind his shoulder, came the evil, voiceless murmuring.

He admits that he passed the end of die avenue at an amble, and was abreast of a semicircle of shrubbery, when a small object was thrust out from the shadow of the bushes, and lay in the open light. Though the night was peculiarly still, it fluttered and balanced a moment, as if windblown, then came in skimming flights to his feet. He picked it up and made for the door, which yielded to his hand, and he flung it to and bolted it behind him.

Once in the warmly-lit hall his senses returned, and he waited to recover breath and composure before facing the two men whose voices and laughter came from the room on his right. But the door of the room was thrown open, and the burly figure of Harland in his shirt- sleeves appeared on the threshold.

'Hullo, Jones, that you? Come along!' he said genially.

'Bless me!' exclaimed Nare-Jones irritably, 'there's not a light in any of the windows. It might be a house of the dead!'

Harland stared at him, but all he said was: 'Have a whisky-and-soda?'

Savelsan, who was leaning over the billiard table, trying side-strokes with his back to Nare-Jones, added:

'Did you expect us to illuminate the place for you? There's not a soul in the house but ourselves.'

'Say when,' said Harland, poising the bottle over a glass.

Nare-Jones laid down what he held in his hand on the corner of the billiard table, and took up his glass.

'What in creation's this?' asked Savelsan.

'I don't know; the wind blew it to my feet just outside,' replied Nare-Jones, between two long pulls at the whisky-and-soda.

'*Blown* to your feet?' repeated Savelsan, taking up the thing and weighing it in his hand. 'It must be blowing a hurricane then.'

'It isn't blowing at all,' returned Nare-Jones blankly. 'The night is dead calm.'

For the object that had fluttered and rolled so lightly across the turf and gravel was a small battered, metal calf, made of some heavy brass amalgam.

Savelsan looked incredulously into Nare-Jones' face, and laughed.

'What's wrong with you? You look queer.'

Nare-Jones laughed too; he was already ashamed of the last ten minutes.

Harland was meantime examining the metal calf.

'It's a Bengali image,' he said, 'It's been knocked about a good bit, by Jove! You say it blew out of the shrubbery?'

'Like a bit of paper, I give you my word, though there was not a breath of wind going,' admitted Nare-Joncs.

'Seems odd, don't yet know?' remarked Harland carelessly, 'Now you two fellows had better begin; I'll mark.'

Nare-Jones happened to be in form that night, and Savelsan became absorbed in the delightful difficulty of giving him a sound thrashing.

Suddenly Savelsan paused in his stroke.

'What's the sin's that?' he asked.

They stood listening. A thin, broken crying could be heard.

'Sounds like green plover,' remarked Nare-Jones chalking his cue.

'It's a kitten they've shut up somewhere,' said Harland.

'That's a child, and in the deuce of a fright, too,' said Savelsan. 'You'd better go and tuck it up in its little bed, Harland,' he added, with a laugh.

Harland opened the door. There could no longer be any doubt about the sounds; the stifled shrieks and thin whimpering told of a child in the extremity of pain and fear.

'It's upstairs,' said Harland. 'I'm going to see.'

Nare-Jones picked up a lamp and followed him.

'I stay here,' said Savelsan sitting down by the fire.

In the hall the two men stopped and listened again. It is hard to locate a noise, but this seemed to come from the upper landing.

'Poor little beggar!' exclaimed Harland, as he bounded up the staircase. The bedroom doors opening on the square central landing above were all locked, the keys being on the outside. But the crying led them into a side passage which ended in a single room.

'It's in here, and the door's locked,' said Nare-Jones. 'Call out and see who's there.'

But Harland was set on business. He flung his weight against the panel, and the door burst open, the lock ricochetting noisily into a corner. As they passed in, the crying ceased abruptly.

Harland stood in the centre of the room, while Nare-Jones held up the light to look round.

'The dickens!' exclaimed Harland exhaustively

The room was entirely empty.

Not so much as a cupboard broke the smooth surface of the walls, only the two low windows and the door by which they had entered.

'This is the room above the billiard-room, isn't it?' said Nare-Jones at last.

'Yes. This is the only one I have not had furnished yet. I thought I might—?

He stopped short, for behind them burst out a peal of harsh, mocking laughter, that rang and echoed between the bare walls.

Both men swung round simultaneously, and both caught a glimpse of a tall, thin figure in black, rocking with laughter in the doorway, but when they turned it was gone. They dashed out into the passage and landing. No one was to be seen. The doors were locked as before, and the staircase and hall were vacant.

After making a prolonged search through every corner of the house, they went back to Savelsan in the billiard-room.

'What were you laughing about? What is it anyway?' began Savelsan at once.

'It's nothing. And we didn't laugh,' replied Nare-Jones definitely.

'But I heard you,' insisted Savelsan. 'And where's the child?'

'I wish you'd go up and find it,' returned Harland grimly, 'We heard the laughing and saw, or thought we saw, a man in black—'

'Something like a priest in a cassock,' put in Nare-Jones.

'Yes, like a priest,' assented Harland, 'but as we turned he disappeared.'

Savelsan sat down and gazed from one to the other of his companions.

'The house behaves as if it was haunted,' he remarked; 'only there is no such thing as an authenticated ghost outside the experiences of the Psychical Research Society. I'd ask the Society down if I were you, Harland. You never can tell what you may find in these old houses.'

'It's not an old house,' replied Harland. 'It was built somewhere about '40. I certainly saw that man; and, look to it, Savelsan, I'll find out who or what he is. That I swear! The English law makes no allowance for ghosts—nor will I.'

'You'll have your hands full, or I'm mistaken,' exclaimed Savelsan, grinning. 'A ghost that laughs and cries in a breath, and rolls battered images about your front door, is not to be trifled with. The night is young yet—not much past eleven. I vote for a peg all round and then I'll finish off Jones.'

Harland, sunk in a fit of sullen abstraction, sat on a settee, and watched them. On a sudden he said:

'It's turned beastly cold.'

'There's a beastly smell, you mean,' corrected Savelsan crossly as he went round the table. He had made a break of forty and did not want to be interrupted. 'The draught is from the window.'

'I've not noticed it before this evening,' said Harland, as he opened the shutters to make sure.

As he did so the night air rushed in heavy with the smell as of an old well that has not been uncovered for years, a smell of slime and unwholesome wetness. The lower part of the window was wide open and Harland banged it down.

'It's abomible!' he said, with an angry sniff. 'Enough to give us all typhoid.'

'Only dead leaves,' remarked Nare-Jones. 'There are the rotten leaves of twenty winters under the trees and outside this window. I noticed them when we came over on Tuesday.'

'I'll have them cleared away tomorrow. I wonder how Thomas came to leave this window open,' grumbled Harland, as he closed and bolted the shutter. 'What do you say—forty-five?' and he went over to mark it up.

The game went on for some time, and Nare-Jones was lying across the table with the cue poised, when he heard a slight sound behind him. Looking round he saw Harland, his face flushed and angry, passing softly—wonderfully softly for so big a man, Nare-Jones remembers thinking—along the angle of the wall towards the window.

All three men unite in declaring that they were watching the shutter, which opened inwards as if thrust by some furtive hand from outside. At the moment Nare-Jones and Savelsan were standing directly opposite to it on the further side of the table, while Harland crouched behind the shutter intent on giving the intruder a lesson.

As the shutter unfolded to its utmost the two men opposite saw a face pressed against the glass, a furrowed evil face, with a wide laugh perched upon its sinister features.

There was a second of absolute stillness, and Nare-Jones' eyes met those other eyes with the fascinated horror of a mutual understanding, as all the foul fancies that had pursued him in the avenue poured back into his mind.

With an uncontrollable impulse of resentment, he snatched a billiard ball from the table and flung it with all his strength at the face. The ball crashed through the glass and through the face beyond it! The glass fell shattered, but the face remained for an instant peering and grinning at the aperture, then as Harland sprang forward it was gone.

'The ball went clean through it!' said Savelsan with a gasp.

They crowded to the window, and throwing up the sash, leant out. The dank smell clung about the air, a boat-shaped moon glimmered between the bare branches, and on the white drive beyond the shrubbery the billiard ball could be seen a shining spot under the moon. Noting more.

'What was it?' asked Harland.

'Only a face at the window,' quoted Savelsan with an awkward attempt at making light of his own scare. 'Devilish queer face too, eh, Jones?'

'I wish I'd got him!' returned Harland frowning. 'I'm not going to put up with any tricks about the place, don't yer know?'

'You'd bottle any tramp loafing around,' said Nare-Jones.

Harland looked down at his immense arms outlined in his shirt- sleeves.

'I could that,' he answered. 'But this chap—did you hit him?'

'Clean through the face! Or, at any rate, it looked like it,' replied Savelsan, as Nare-Jones stood silent.

Harland shut the shutter and poked up the fire.

'It's a cursed creepy affair!' he said, 'I hope the servants won't get hold of this nonsense. Ghosts play the very mischief with a house. Though I don't believe in them myself,' he concluded.

Then Savelsan broke out in an unexpected place.

'Nor do I—as a rule,' he said slowly. 'Still, you know it is a sickening idea to think of a spirit condemned to haunt the scene of its crime waiting for the world to die.'

Harland and Nare-Jones looked at him.

'Have a whisky neat,' suggested Harland, soothingly. 'I never knew you taken that way before.'

Nare-Jones laughed out. He says he does not know why he laughed nor why he said what follows.

'It's this way,' he said. 'The moment of foul satisfaction is gone for ever, yet for all time the guilty spirit must perpetuate its sin— the sin that brought no lasting reward, only a momentary reward experienced, it may be, centuries ago, but to which still clings the punishment of eternally rehearsing in loneliness, and cold, and gloom, the sin of other days. No punishment can be conceived more horrible. Savelsan is right.'

'I think we've had enough about ghosts,' said Harland, cheerfully, 'let's go on. Hurry up, Savelsan.'

'There's the billiard ball,' said Nare-Jones. 'Who'll go fetch?'

'Not I,' replied Savelsan promptly. 'When that—was at the window, I felt sick.'

Nare-Jones nodded. 'And I wanted to bolt!' he said emphatically.

Harland faced about from the fire.

'And I, though I saw nothing but the shutter, I—hang it!—don't yet know—so did I! There was panic in the air for a minute. But I'm shot if I'm afraid now,' he concluded doggedly, 'I'll go.'

His heavy animal face was lit with courage and resolution.

'I've spent close upon five thousand pounds over this blessed house first and last, and I'm not going to be done out of it by any infernal spiritualism!' he added, as he took down his coat and pulled it on.

'It's all in view from the window except those few yards through the shrubbery,' said Savelsan. 'Take a stick and go. Though, on second thoughts, I bet you a fiver you don't.'

'I don't want a stick,' answered Harland. 'I'm not afraid—not now—and I'd meet most men with my hands.'

Nare-Jones opened the shutters again; the sash was low and he pushed die window up, and leant far out.

'It's not much of a drop,' he said, and slung his legs out over the lintel; but the night was full of the smell, and something else. He leapt back into the room. 'Don't go, Harland!'

Harland gave him a look that set his blood burning.

'What is there, after all, to be afraid of in a ghost?' he asked heavily.

Nare-Jones, sick with the sense of his own newly-born cowardice, yet entirely unable to master it, answered feebly:

'I can't say, but don't go.'

The words seemed inevitable, though he could have kicked himself for hanging back.

There was a forced laugh from Savelsan.

'Give it up and stop at home, little man,' he said.

Harland merely snorted in reply, and laid his great leg over the window ledge. The other two watched his big, tweed-clad figure as it crossed the grass and disappeared into the shrubbery.

'You and I are in a preposterous funk,' said Savelsan, with unpleasant explicitness, as Harland, whistling loudly, passed into the shadow.

But this was a point on which Nare-Jones could not bring himself to speak at the moment. Then they sat on the sill and waited. The moon shone out clearly above the avenue, which now lay white and undimmed between its crowding trees.

'And he's whistling because he's afraid,' continued Savelsan.

'He's not often afraid,' replied Nare-Jones shortly; 'besides, he's doing what neither of us were very keen on.'

The whistling stopped suddenly. Savelsan said afterwards that he fancied he saw Harland's huge, grey-clad shoulders, with uplifted arms, rise for a second above the bushes.

Then out of the silence came peal upon peal of that infernal laughter, and, following it, the thin pitiful crying of the child. That too ceased, and an absolute stillness seemed to fall upon the place.

They leant out and listened intently. The minutes passed slowly. In the middle of the avenue the billiard ball glinted on the gravel, but there was no sign of Harland emerging from the shrubbery path.

'He should be there by now,' said Nare-Jones anxiously.

They listened again; everything was quiet. The ticking of Harland's big watch on the mantelpiece was distinctly audible.

'This is too much,' said Nare-Jones. 'I'm going to see where he is.'

He swung himself out on the grass, and Savelsan called to him to wait, as he was coming also. While Nare-Jones stood waiting, there was a sound as of a pig grunting and rooting among the dead leaves in the shrubbery.

They ran forward into the darkness, and found the shrubbery path. A minute later they came upon something that tossed and snorted and rolled under the shrubs.

'Great Heavens!' cried Nare-Jones, 'it's Harland!'

'He's breaking somebody's neck,' added Savelsan, peering into the gloom.

Nare-Jones was himself again. The powerful instinct of his profession—the help-giving instinct, possessed him to the exclusion of every other feeling.

'He's in a fit—just a fit,' he said in matter of fact tones, as he bent over the struggling form; 'that's all.'

With the assistance of Savelsan, he managed to carry Harland out into the open drive. Harland's eyes were fearful, and froth hung about his blue puffing lips as they laid him down upon the ground. He rolled over, and lay still, while from the shadows broke another shout of laughter.

'It's apoplexy. We must get him away from here,' said Nare-Jones. 'But, first, I'm going to see what is in those bushes.'

He dashed through the shrubbery, backwards and forwards. He seemed to feel the strength of ten men as he wrenched and tore and trampled the branches, letting in the light of the moon to its darkness. At last he paused, exhausted.

'Of course, there's nothing,' said Savelsan wearily. 'What did you expect after the incident of the billiard ball?'

Together, with awful toil, they bore the big man down the narrow avenue, and at the lodge gates they met the carriage.

Some time later the subject of their common experiences at Medhans Lea was discussed amongst the three men. Indeed, for many weeks Harland had not been in a state to discuss any subject at all, but as soon as he was allowed to do so, he invited Nare-Jones and Savelsan to meet Mr Flaxman Low, the scientist, whose works on psychology and kindred matters are so well known at the Metropole, to thresh out the matter.

Flaxman Low listened with his usual air of gentle abstraction, from time to time making notes on the back of an envelope. He looked at each narrator in turn as he took up the thread of the story. He understood perfectly that the man who stood furthest from the mystery must inevitably have been the self-centred Savelsan; next in order came Nare-Jones, with sympathetic possibilities, but a crowded brain; closest of all would be big, kindly Harland, with more than one strong animal instinct about him, and whose bulk of matter was evidently permeated by a receptive spirit.

When they had ended, Savelsan turned to Flaxman Low.

'There you have the events, Mr Low. Now, the question is how to deal with them.'

'Classify them,' replied Flaxman Low.

'The crying would seem to indicate a child,' began Savelsan, ticking off the list on his fingers; 'the black figure, the face at the window, and the laughter are naturally connected. So far I can go alone. I conclude that we saw the apparition of a man, possibly a priest, who had during his lifetime illtreated a child, and whose punishment it is to haunt the scene of his crime.'

'Precisely—the punishment being worked out under conditions which admit of human observation,' returned Flaxman Low. 'As for the child the sound of crying was merely part of the *mise-en-scene*. The child was not there.'

'But that explanation stops short of several points. Now about the suggestive thoughts experienced by my friend, Nare-Jones; what brought on the fit in the case of Mr Harland, who assures us that he was not suffering from fright or other violent emotion; and what connection can be traced between all these things and the Bengali image?' Savelsan ended.

'Let us take the Bengali figure first,' said Low. 'it is just one of those discrepant particulars which, at first sight, seem wholly irreconcilable with the rest of the phenomena, yet these often form a test point, by which our theories are proved or otherwise.' Flaxman Low took up the metal calf from the table as he spoke. 'I should be inclined to connect this with the child. Observe it. It has not been roughly used; it is rubbed and dinted as a plaything usually is. I should say the child may have had Anglo-Indian relations.'

At this, Nare-Jones bent forward, and in his turn examined the figure, while Savelsan smiled his thin, incredulous smile.

'These are ingenious theories,' he said; 'but we are realty no nearer to facts, I am afraid.'

'The only proof would be an inquiry into the former history of Medhans Lea; if events had happened there which would go to support this theory, why, then—But I cannot supply that information since I never heard of Medhans Lea or the ghost until I entered this room.'

'I know something of Medhans Lea,' put in Nare-Jones. 'I found out a good deal about it before I left the place. And I must congratulate Mr Low on his methods, for his theory tallies in a wonderful manner with the facts of the case. The house was long known to be haunted. It seems that many years ago a lady, the widow of an Indian officer, lived there with her only child, a boy, for whom she engaged a tutor, a dark-looking man, who wore a long black coat like a cassock, and was called 'the Jesuit' by the country people.

'One evening the man took the boy out into the shrubbery. Screams were heard, and when the child was brought in he was found to have lost his reason. He used to cry and shriek incessantly, but was never able to tell what had been done to him as long as he lived. As for this metal calf, the mother probably brought it with her from India, and the child used it as a toy, perhaps, because he was allowed no others. Hullo' In handling the calf, Nare-Jones had touched some hidden spring, the head opened, disclosing a small cavity, from which dropped a little ring of blue beads, such as children make. He held it up. 'This affords good proof.'

'Yes,' admitted Savelsan grudgingly. 'But how about your sensations and Harland's seizure? You must know what was done to the child, Harland—what did you see in the shrubbery?'

Harland's florid face assumed a queer pallor.

'I saw something,' replied he hesitatingly, 'but I can't recall what it was. I only remember being possessed by a blind terror, and then nothing more until I recovered consciousness at the hotel next day.' 'Can you account for this, Mr Low?' asked Nare-Jones, 'and there was also my strange notion of the whispering in the avenue.'

'I think so,' replied Flaxman Low. 'I believe that the theory of atmospheric influences, which includes the power of environment to reproduce certain scenes and also thoughts, would throw light upon your sensations as well as Mr Harland's. Such influences play a far larger part in our everyday experience than we have as yet any idea of.'

There was a silence of a few moments; then Harland spoke:

'I fancy that we have said all that there is to be said upon the matter. We are much obliged to you, Mr Low. I don't know how it strikes you other fellows, but, speaking for myself, I have seen enough of ghosts to last me for a very long time.'

'And now,' ended Harland wearily,' if you have no objections, we will pass on to pleasanter subjects.'

At The Pit's Mouth

By Rudyard Kipling

Once upon a time there was a Man and his Wife and a Tertium Quid.

All three were unwise, but the Wife was the unwisest. The Man should have looked after his Wife, who should have avoided the Tertium Quid, who, again, should have married a wife of his own, after clean and open flirtations, to which nobody can possibly object, round Jakko or Observatory Hill. When you see a young man with his pony in a white lather, and his hat on the back of his head flying down-hill at fifteen miles an hour to meet a girl who will be properly surprised to meet him, you naturally approve of that young man, and wish him Staff appointments, and take an interest in his welfare, and, as the proper time comes, give them sugar-tongs or side-saddles according to your means and generosity.

The Tertium Quid flew down-hill on horseback, but it was to meet the Man's Wife; and when he flew up-hill it was for the same end. The Man was in the Plains, earning money for the Wife to spend on dresses and four-hundred-rupee bracelets, and inexpensive luxuries of that kind. He worked very hard, and sent her a letter or a postcard daily. She also wrote to him daily, and said that she was longing for him to come up to Simla. The Tertium Quid used to lean over her shoulder and laugh as she wrote the notes. Then the two would ride to the Post-office together.

Now, Simla is a strange place and its customs are peculiar; nor is any man who has not spent at least ten seasons there qualified to pass judgment on circumstantial evidence, which is the most untrustworthy in the Courts. For these reasons, and for others which need not appear, I decline to state positively whether there was anything irretrievably wrong in the relations between the Man's Wife and the Tertium Quid. If there was, and hereon you must form your own opinion, it was the Man's Wife's fault. She was kittenish in her manners, wearing generally an air of soft and fluffy innocence. But she was deadlily learned and evil-instructed; and, now and again, when the mask dropped, men saw this, shuddered and—almost drew back. Men are occasionally particular, and the least particular men are always the most exacting.

Simla is eccentric in its fashion of treating friendships. Certain attachments which have set and crystallized through half a dozen seasons acquire almost the sanctity of the marriage bond, and are revered as such. Again, certain attachments equally old, and, to all appearance, equally venerable, never seem to win any recognized official status; while a chance-sprung acquaintance, not two months born, steps into the place which by right belongs to the senior. There is no law reducible to print which regulates these affairs.

Some people have a gift which secures them infinite toleration, and others have not. The Man's Wife had not. If she looked over the garden wait, for instance, women taxed her with stealing their husbands. She complained pathetically that she was not allowed to choose her own friends. When she put up her big white muff to her lips, and gazed over it and under her eyebrows at you as she said this thing, you felt that she had been infamously misjudged, and that all the other women's instincts were all wrong; which was absurd. She was not allowed to own the Tertium Quid in peace; and was so strangely constructed that she would not have enjoyed peace had she been so permitted. She preferred some semblance of intrigue to cloak even her most commonplace actions.

After two months of riding, first round Jakko, then Elysium, then Summer Hill, then Observatory Hill, then under Jutogh, and lastly up and down the Cart Road as far as the Tara Devi gap in the dusk, she said to the Tertium Quid, 'Frank, people say we are too much together, and people are so horrid.'

The Tertium Quid pulled his moustache, and replied that horrid people were unworthy of the consideration of nice people.

'But they have done more than talk—they have written—written to my hubby—I'm sure of it,' said the Man's Wife, and she pulled a letter from her husband out of her saddle-pocket and gave it to the Tertium Quid.

It was an honest letter, written by an honest man, then stewing in the Plains on two hundred rupees a month (for he allowed his wife eight hundred and fifty), and in a silk banian and cotton trousers. It is said that, perhaps, she had not thought of the unwisdom of allowing her name to be so generally coupled with the Tertium Quid's; that she was too much of a child to understand the dangers of that sort of thing; that he, her husband, was the last man in the world to interfere jealously with her little amusements and interests, but that it would be better were she to drop the Tertium Quid quietly and for her husband's sake. The letter was sweetened with many pretty little pet names, and it amused the Tertium Quid considerably. He and She laughed over it, so that you, fifty yards away, could see their shoulders shaking while the horses slouched along side by side.

Their conversation was not worth reporting. The upshot of it was that, next day, no one saw the Man's Wife and the Tertium Quid together. They had both gone down to the Cemetery, which, as a rule, is only visited officially by the inhabitants of Simla.

A Simla funeral with the clergyman riding, the mourners riding, and the coffin creaking as it swings between the bearers, is one of the most depressing things on this earth, particularly when the procession passes under the wet, dank dip beneath the Rockcliffe Hotel, where the sun is shut out, and all the hill streams are wailing and weeping together as they go down the valleys.

Occasionally, folk tend the graves, but we in India shift and are transferred so often that, at the end of the second year, the Dead have no friends—only acquaintances who are far too busy amusing themselves up the hill to attend to old partners. The idea of using a Cemetery as a rendezvous is distinctly a feminine one. A man would have said simply, 'Let people talk. We'll go down the Mall.' A woman is made differently, especially if she be such a woman as the Man's Wife. She and the Tertium Quid enjoyed each other's society among the graves of men and women whom they had known and danced with aforetime.

They used to take a big horse-blanket and sit on the grass a little to the left of the lower end, where there is a dip in the ground, and where the occupied graves stop short and the ready-made ones are not ready. Each well-regulated Indian Cemetery keeps half a dozen graves permanently open for contingencies and incidental wear and tear. In the Hills these are more usually baby's size, because children who come up weakened and sick from the Plains often succumb to the effects of the rains in the hills or get pneumonia from their *ayahs* taking them through damp pine-woods after the sun has set. In Cantonments, of course, the man's size is more in request; these arrangements varying with the climate and population.

One day when the Man's Wife and the Tertium Quid had just arrived in the Cemetery, they saw some coolies breaking ground. They had marked out a full-size grave, and the Tertium Quid asked them whether any *Sahib* was sick. They said that they did not know; but it was an order that they should dig a *Sahib's* grave.

'Work away,' said the Tertium Quid, 'and let's see how it's done.

The coolies worked away, and the Man's Wife and the Tertium Quid watched and talked for a couple of hours while the grave was being deepened. Then a coolie, taking the earth in baskets as it was thrown up, jumped over the grave.

'That's queer,' said the Tertium Quid. 'Where's my ulster?'

'What's queer?' said the Man's Wife.

'I have got a chill down my back—just as if a goose had walked over my grave.'

'Why do you look at the thing, then?' said the Man's Wife. 'Let us go.'

The Tertium Quid stood at the head of the grave, and stared without answering for a space. Then he said, dropping a pebble down, 'It is nasty—and cold: horribly cold. I don't think I shall come to the Cemetery anymore. I don't think grave-digging is cheerful.'

The two talked and agreed that the Cemetery was depressing. They also arranged for a ride next day out from the Cemetery through the Mashobra Tunnel up to Fagoo and back, because all the world was going to a garden-party at Viceregal Lodge, and all the people of Mashobra would go too.

Coming up the Cemetery road, the Tertium Quid's horse tried to bolt up-hill, being tired with standing so long, and managed to strain a back sinew.

'I shall have to take the mare tomorrow,' said the Tertium Quid, 'and she will stand nothing heavier than a snaffle.'

They made their arrangements to meet in the Cemetery, after allowing all the Mashobra people time to pass into Simla. That night it rained heavily, and, next day, when the Tertium Quid came to the trysting-place, he saw that the new grave had a foot of water in it, the ground being a tough and sour clay.

'Jove! That looks beastly,' said the Tertium Quid. 'Fancy being boarded up and dropped into that well!'

They then started off to Fagoo, the mare playing with the snaffle and picking her way as though she were shod with satin, and the sun shining divinely. The road below Mashobra to Fagoo is officially styled the Himalayan-Thibet Road; but in spite of its name it is not much more than six feet wide in most places, and the drop into the valley below may be anything between one and two thousand feet.

'Now we're going to Thibet,' said the Man's Wife merrily, as the horses drew near to Fagoo. She was riding on the cliff-side.

'Into Thibet,' said the Tertium Quid, 'ever so far from people who say horrid things, and hubbies who write stupid letters. With you—to the end of the world!'

A coolie carrying a log of wood came round a corner, and the mare went wide to avoid him—forefeet in and haunches out, as a sensible mare should go.

'To the world's end,' said the Man's Wife, and looked unspeakable things over her near shoulder at the Tertium Quid.

He was smiling, but, while she looked, the smile froze stiff as it were on his face, and changed to a nervous grin—the sort of grin men wear when they are not quite easy in their saddles. The mare seemed to be sinking by the stern, and her nostrils cracked while she was trying to realize what was happening. The rain of the night before had rotted the drop-side of the Himalayan-Thibet Road, and it was giving way under her. 'What are you doing?' said the Man's Wife. The Tertium Quid gave no answer. He grinned nervously and set his spurs into the mare, who rapped with her forefeet on the road, and the struggle began. The Man's Wife screamed, 'Oh, Frank, get off!'

But the Tertium Quid was glued to the saddle—his face blue and white—and he looked into the Man's Wife's eyes. Then the Man's Wife clutched at the mare's head and caught her by the nose instead of the bridle. The brute threw up her head and went down with a scream, the Tertium Quid upon her, and the nervous grin still set on his face.

The Man's Wife heard the tinkle-tinkle of little stones and loose earth falling off the roadway, and the sliding roar of the man and horse going down. Then everything was quiet, and she called on Frank to leave his mare and walk up. But Frank did not answer. He was underneath the mare, nine hundred feet below, spoiling a patch of Indian corn.

As the revellers came back from Viceregal Lodge in the mists of the evening, they met a temporarily insane woman, on a temporarily mad horse, swinging round the corners, with her eyes and her mouth open, and her head like the head of a Medusa. She was stopped by a man at the risk of his life, and taken out of the saddle, a limp heap, and put on the bank to explain herself. This wasted twenty minutes, and then she was sent home in a lady's rickshaw, still with her mouth open and her hands picking at her riding-gloves.

She was in bed through the following three days, which were rainy; so she missed attending the funeral of the Tertium Quid, who was lowered into eighteen inches of water, instead of the twelve to which he had first objected.

The Dead Man of Varley Grange

A Victorian Ghost Story... Author Unknown

'Hallo, Jack! Where are you off to? Going down to the governor's place for Christmas?'

Jack Darent, who was in my old regiment, stood drawing on his dogskin gloves upon 23 December the year before last. He was equipped in a long Ulster and top hat, and a hansom, already loaded with a gun-case and portmanteau, stood awaiting him. He had a tall, strong figure, a fair, fresh-looking face, and the merriest blue eyes in the world. He held a cigarette between his lips, and late as was the season of the year there was a flower in his buttonhole. "When did I ever see handsome Jack Darent and he did not look well dressed and well fed and jaunty?" As I ran up the steps of the Club he turned round and laughed merrily.

'My dear fellow, do I look the sort of man to be victimized at a family Christmas meeting? Do you know the kind of business they have at home? Three maiden aunts and a bachelor uncle, my eldest brother and his insipid wife, and all my sister's six noisy children at dinner. Church twice a day, and snap-dragon between the services! No, thank you! I have a great affection for my old parents, but you don't catch me going in for that sort of national festival!'

'You irreverent ruffian!' I replied, laughing. 'Ah, if you were a married man——'

'Ah, if I were a married man!' replied Captain Darent with something that was almost a sigh, and then, lowering his voice, he said hurriedly, 'How is Miss Lester, Fred?'

'My sister is quite well, thank you,' I answered with becoming gravity; and it was not without a spice of malice that I added, 'She has been going out to a great many balls and enjoying herself very much.'

Captain Darent looked profoundly miserable.

'I don't see how a poor fellow in a marching regiment, a younger son too, with nothing in the future to look to, is ever to marry nowadays,' he said almost savagely; 'when girls, too, are used to so much luxury and extravagance that they can't live without it. Matrimony is at a deadlock in this century, Fred, chiefly owing to the price of butchers' meat and bonnets. In fifty years' time it will become extinct and the country be depopulated. But I must be off, old man, or I shall miss my train.'

'You have never told me where you are going to, Jack.'

'Oh, I am going to stay with old Henderson, in Westernshire; he has taken a furnished house, with some first-rate pheasant shooting, for a year. There are seven of us going—all bachelors, and all kindred spirits. We shall shoot all day and smoke half the night. Think what you have lost, old fellow, by becoming a Benedick!'

'In Westernshire, is it?' I inquired. 'Whereabouts is this place, and what is the name of it? For I am a Westernshire man by birth myself, and I know every place in the county.'

'Oh, it's a tumbledown sort of old house, I believe,' answered Jack carelessly. 'Gables and twisted chimneys outside, and uncomfortable spindle-legged furniture inside—you know the sort of thing; but the shooting is capital, Henderson says, and we must put up with our quarters. He has taken his French cook down, and plenty of liquor, so I've no doubt we shan't starve.'

'Well, but what is the name of it?' I persisted, with a growing interest in the subject.

'Let me see,' referring to a letter he pulled out of his pocket. 'Oh, here it is—Varley Grange.'

'Varley Grange!' I repeated, aghast. 'Why, it has not been inhabited for years.'

'I believe not,' answered Jack unconcernedly. 'The shooting has been let separately; but Henderson took a fancy to the house too and thought it would do for him, furniture and all, just as it is. My dear Fred, what are you looking so solemnly at me for?'

'Jack, let me entreat of you not to go to this place,' I said, laying my hand on his arm.

'Not go! Why, Lester, you must be mad! Why on earth shouldn't I go there?'

'There are stories—uncomfortable things said of that house.' I had not the moral courage to say, 'It is haunted,' and I felt myself how weak and childish was my attempt to deter him from his intended visit; only—I knew all about Varley Grange.

I think handsome Jack Darent thought privately that I was slightly out of my senses, for I am sure I looked unaccountably upset and dismayed by the mention of the name of the house that Mr Henderson had taken.

'I daresay it's cold and draughty and infested with rats and mice,' he said laughingly; 'and I have no doubt the creature-comforts will not be equal to Queen's Gate; but I stand pledged to go now, and I must be off this very minute, so have no time, old fellow, to inquire into the meaning of your sensational warning. Goodbye, and—and remember me to the ladies.'

He ran down the steps and jumped into the hansom.

'Write to me if you have time!' I cried out after him; but I don't think he heard me in the rattle of the departing cab. He nodded and smiled at me and was swiftly whirled out of sight.

As for me, I walked slowly back to my comfortable house in Queen's Gate. There was my wife presiding at the little five o'clock tea-table, our two fat, pink and white little children tumbling about upon the hearthrug amongst dolls and bricks, and two utterly spoilt and overfed pugs; and my sister Bella—who, between ourselves, was the prettiest as well as dearest girl in all London—sitting on the floor in her handsome brown velvet gown, resigning herself gracefully to be trampled upon by the dogs, and to have her hair pulled by the babies.

'Why, Fred, you look as if you had heard bad news,' said my wife, looking up anxiously as I entered.

'I don't know that I have heard of anything very bad; I have just seen Jack Darent off for Christmas,' I said, turning instinctively towards my sister. He was a poor man and a younger son, and of course a very bad match for the beautiful Miss Lester; but for all that I had an inkling that Bella was not quite indifferent to her brother's friend.

'Oh!' says that hypocrite. 'Shall I give you a cup of tea, Fred?'

It is wonderful how women can control their faces and pretend not to care a straw when they hear the name of their lover mentioned. I think Bella overdid it, she looked so supremely indifferent.

'Where on earth do you suppose he is going to stay, Bella?'

'Who? Oh, Captain Darent! How should I possibly know where he is going? Archie, pet, please don't poke the doll's head quite down Ponto's throat; I know he will bite it off if you do.'

This last observation was addressed to my son and heir.

'Well, I think you will be surprised when you hear, he is going to Westernshire, to stay at Varley Grange.'

'*What!*' No doubt about her interest in the subject now! Miss Lester turned as white as her collar and sprang to her feet impetuously, scattering dogs, babies and toys in all directions away from her skirts as she rose.

'You cannot mean it, Fred! Varley Grange, why, it has not been inhabited for ten years; and the last time—— Oh, do you remember those poor people who took it? What a terrible story it has!' She shuddered.

'Well, it is taken now' I said, 'by a man I know, called Henderson—a bachelor; he has asked down a party of men for a week's shooting, and Jack Darent is one of them.'

'For Heaven's sake prevent him from going!' cried Bella, clasping her hands.

'My dear, he is gone!'

'Oh, then write to him—telegraph—tell him to come back!' she urged breathlessly.

'I am afraid it is no use,' I said gravely. 'He would not come back; he would not believe me; he would think I was mad.'

'Did you tell him anything?' she asked faintly.

'No, I had no time. I did say a word or two, but he began to laugh.'

'Yes, that is how it always is!' she said distractedly. 'People laugh and pooh-pooh the whole thing, and then they go there and see for themselves, and it is too late!'

She was so thoroughly upset that she left the room. My wife turned to me in astonishment; not being a Westernshire woman, she was not well up in the traditions of that venerable county.

'What on earth does it all mean, Fred?' she asked me in amazement. 'What is the matter with Bella, and why is she so distressed that, Captain Darent is going to stay at that particular house?'

'It is said to be haunted, and——'

'You don't mean to say you believe in such rubbish, Fred?' interrupted my wife sternly with a side-glance of apprehension at our first-born who, needless to say, stood by, all eyes and ears, drinking in every word of the conversation of his elders.

'I never know what I believe or what I don't believe,' I answered gravely. 'All I can say is that there are very singular traditions about that house, and that a great many credible witnesses have seen a very strange thing there, and that a great many disasters have happened to the persons who have seen it.'

'What has been seen, Fred? Pray tell me the story! Wait, I think I will send the children away.'

My wife rang the bell for the nurse, and as soon as the little ones had been taken from the room she turned to me again.

'I don't believe in ghosts or any such rubbish one bit, but I should like to hear your story.'

'The story is vague enough,' I answered.

'In the old days Varley Grange belonged to the ancient family of Varley, now completely extinct. There was, some hundred years ago, a daughter, famed for her beauty and her fascination. She wanted to marry a poor, penniless squire, who loved her devotedly Her hrother, Dennis Varky, the new owner of Varley Grange, refused his consent and shut his sister up in the nunnery that used to stand outside his park gates—there are a few ruins of it left still. The poor nun broke her vows and ran away in the night with her lover. But her brother pursued her and brought her back with him. The lover escaped, but the lord of Varley murdered his sister under his own roof, swearing that no scion of his race should live to disgrace and dishonour his ancient name.

'Ever since that day Dennis Varley's spirit cannot rest in its grave—he wanders about the old house at night-time, and those who have seen him are numberless. Now and then the pale, shadowy form of a nun flits across the old hall, or along the gloomy passages, and when both strange shapes are seen thus together misfortune and illness, and even death, is sure to pursue the luckless man who has seen them, with remorseless cruelty.'

'I wonder you believe in such rubbish,' says my wife at the conclusion of my tale.

I shrug my shoulders and answer nothing, for who are so obstinate as those who persist in disbelieving everything that they cannot understand?

It was little more than a week later that, walking by myself along Pall Mall one afternoon, I suddenly came upon Jack Darent walking towards me.

'Hallo, Jack! Back again? Why, man, how odd you look!'

There was a change in the man that I was instantly aware of. His frank, careless face looked clouded and anxious, and the merry smile was missing from his handsome countenance.

'Come into the Club, Fred,' he said, taking me by the arm. 'I have something to say to you.'

He drew me into a corner of the Club smoking-room.

'You were quite right. I wish to Heaven I had never gone to that house.'

'You mean—have you seen anything?' I inquired eagerly

'I have seen *everything*,' he answered with a shudder. 'They say one dies within a year——'

'My dear fellow, don't be-so upset about it,' I interrupted; I was quite distressed to see how thoroughly the man had altered.

'Let me tell you about it, Fred.'

He drew his chair close to mine and told me his story, pretty nearly in the following words:

'You remember the day I went down you had kept me talking at the Club door; I had a race to catch the train; however, I just did it. I found the other fellows all waiting for me. There was Charlie Wells, the two Harfords, old Colonel Riddell, who is such a crack shot, two fellows in the Guards, both pretty fair, a man called Thompson, a barrister, Henderson and myself—eight of us in all. We had a remarkably lively journey down, as you may imagine, and reached Varley Grange in the highest possible spirits. We all slept like tops that night.

'The next day we were out from eleven till dusk among the coverts, and a better day's shooting I never enjoyed in the whole course of my life, the birds literally swarmed. We bagged a hundred and thirty brace. We were all pretty well tired when we got home, and did full justice to a very good dinner and first-class Perrier-Jouet. After dinner we adjourned to the hall to smoke. This hall is quite the feature of the house. It is large and bright, panelled halfway up with sombre old oak, and vaulted with heavy carved oaken rafters. At the farther end runs a gallery, into which opened the door of my bedroom, and shut off from the rest of the passages by a swing door at either end.

'Well, all we fellows sat up there smoking and drinking brandy and soda, and jawing, you know—as men always do when they are together—about sport of all kinds, hunting and shooting and salmon fishing; and I assure you not one of us had a thought in our heads beyond relating some wonderful incident of a long shot or big fence by which he would each cap the last speaker's experiences. We were just, I recollect, listening to a long story of the old Colonel's, about his experiences among bisons in

Cachemire, when suddenly one of us—I can't remember who it was—gave a sort of shout and started to his feet, pointing up to the gallery behind us. We all turned round, and there—I give you my word of honour, Lester—stood a man leaning over the rail of the gallery, staring down upon us.

'We all saw him. Everyone of us. Eight of us, remember. He stood there full ten seconds, looking down with horrible glittering eyes at us. He had a long tawny beard, and his hands, that were crossed together before him, were nothing but skin and bone. But it was his face that was so unspeakably dreadful. It was livid—the face of a dead man!'

'How was he dressed?'

'I could not see; he wore some kind of a black cloak over his shoulders, I think, but the lower part of his figure was hidden behind the railings. Well, we all stood perfectly speechless for, as I said, about ten seconds; and then the figure moved, backing slowly into the door of the room behind him, which stood open. It was the door of my bedroom! As soon as he had disappeared our senses seemed to return to us. There was a general rush for the staircase, and, as you may imagine, there was not a corner of the house that was left unsearched; my bedroom especially was ransacked in every part of it. But all in vain; there was not the slightest trace to be found of any living being. You may suppose that not one of us slept that night. We lighted every candle and lamp we could lay hands upon and sat up till daylight, but nothing more was seen.

'The next morning, at breakfast, Henderson, who seemed very much annoyed by the whole thing, begged us not to speak of it any more. He said that he had been told, before he had taken the house, that it was supposed to be haunted; but, not being a believer in such childish follies, he had paid but little attention to the rumour. He did not, however, want it talked about, because of the servants, who would be so easily frightened. He was quite certain, he said, that the figure we had seen last night must be somebody dressed up to practise a trick upon us, and he recommended us all to bring our guns down loaded after dinner, but meanwhile to forget the startling apparition as far as we could.

'We, of course, readily agreed to do as he wished, although I do not think that one of us imagined for a moment that any amount of dressing-up would be able to simulate the awful countenance that we had all of us seen too plainly. It would have taken a Hare or an Arthur Cecil, with all the theatrical appliances known only to those two talented actors, to have 'made-up' the face, that was literally that of a corpse. Such a person could not be amongst us— actually in the house—without our knowledge.

'We had another good day's shooting, and by degrees the fresh air and exercise and the excitement of the sport obliterated the impression of what we had seen in some measure from the minds of most of us. That evening we all appeared in the hall after dinner with our loaded guns besides us; but, although we sat up till the small hours and looked frequently up at the gallery at the end of the hall, nothing at all disturbed us that night.

'Two nights thus went by and nothing further was seen of the gentleman with the tawny beard. What with the good company, the good cheer and the pheasants, we had pretty well forgotten all about him.

'We were sitting as usual upon the third night, with our pipes and our cigars; pleasant glow from the bright wood fire in the great chimney lighted up the old hall, and shed a genial warmth about us, when suddenly it seemed to me as if there came a breath of cold, chill air behind me, such as one feels when going down into some damp, cold vault or cellar.

'A strong shiver shook me from head to foot. Before even I saw it I *knew* that It was there.

'It leant over the railing of the gallery and looked down at us all just as it had done before. There was no change in the attitude, no alteration in the fixed, malignant glare in those stony, lifeless eyes; no movement in the white and bloodless features. Below, amongst the eight of us gathered there, there arose a panic of terror. Eight strong, healthy, well-educated nineteenth-century Englishmen, and yet I am not ashamed to say that we were paralyzed with fear. Then one, more quickly recovering his senses than the rest, caught at his gun, that leant against the wide chimney-corner, and fired.

'The hall was filled with smoke, but as it cleared away every one of us could see the figure of our supernatural visitant slowly backing, as he had done on the previous occasion, into the chamber behind him, with something like a sardonic smile of scornful derision upon his horrible, death-like face.

'The next morning it is a singular and remarkable fact that four out of the eight of us received by the morning post—so they stated— letters of importance which called them up to town by the very first train! One man's mother was ill, another had to consult his lawyer, whilst pressing engagements, to which they could assign no definite name, called away the other two.

'There were left in the house that day but four of us—Wells, Bob Harford, our host, and myself. A sort of dogged determination not to be worsted by a scare of this kind kept us still there. The morning light brought a return of common sense and of natural courage to us. We could manage to laugh over last night's terrors whilst discussing our bacon and kidneys and hot coffee over the late breakfast in the pleasant morning-room, with the sunshine streaming cheerily in through the diamond-paned windows.

' "It *must* be a delusion of our brains," said one.

' "Our host's champagne," suggested another.

' "A well-organized hoax," opined a third.

' "I will tell you what we will do," said our host. "Now that those other fellows have all gone—and I suppose we don't any of us believe much in those elaborate family reasons which have so unaccountably summoned them away—we four will sit up regularly night after night and watch for this thing, whatever it may be. I do not believe in ghosts. However, this morning I have taken the trouble to go out before breakfast to see the Rector of the parish, an old gentleman who is well up in all the traditions of the neighbourhood, and I have learnt from him the whole of the supposed story of our friend of the tawny beard, which, if you like, I will relate to you."

'Henderson then proceeded to tell us the tradition concerning the Dennis Varley who murdered his sister, the nun—a story which I will not repeat to you, Lester, as I see you know it already.

'The clergyman had furthermore told him that the figure of the murdered nun was also sometimes seen in the same gallery, but that this as a very rare occurrence. When both murderer and his victim are seen together terrible misfortunes are sure to assail the unfortunate living man who sees them; and if the nun's face is revealed death within the year is the doom of the ill-fated person who has seen it.

' "Of course,' concluded our host, 'I consider all these stories to be absolutely childish. At the same time I cannot help thinking that some human agency—probably a gang of thieves or housebreakers—is at work, and that we shall probably be able to unearth an organized system of villainy by which the rogues, presuming on the credulity of the persons who have inhabited the place, have been able to plant themselves securely among some secret passages and hidden rooms in the house, and have carried on their depredations undiscovered and unsuspected. Now, will all of you help me to unravel this mystery?'

'We all promised readily to do so. It is astonishing how brave we felt at eleven o'clock in the morning; what an amount of pluck and courage each man professed himself to be endued with; how lightly we jested about the 'old boy with the beard,' and what jokes we cracked about the murdered nun!

' "She would show her face oftener if she was good-looking. No fear of her looking at Bob Harford, he was too ugly. It was Jack Darent who was the showman of the party; she'd be sure to make straight for him if she could, he was always run after by the women,' and so on, till we were all laughing loudly and heartily over our own witticisms. That was eleven o'clock in the morning.

'At eleven o'clock at night we could have given a very different report of ourselves.

'At eleven o'clock at night each man took up his appointed post in solemn and somewhat depressed silence.

'The plan of our campaign had been carefully organized by our host. Each man was posted separately with about thirty yards between them, so that no optical delusion, such as an effect of firelight upon the oak panelling, nor any reflection from the circular mirror over the chimney-piece, should be able to deceive more than one of us. Our host fixed himself in the very centre of the hall, facing the gallery at the end; Wells took up his position halfway up the short, straight flight of steps; Harford was at the top of the stairs upon the gallery itself; I was opposite to him at the further end. In this manner, whenever the figure—ghost or burglar—should appear, it must necessarily be between two of us, and be seen from both the right and the left side. We were prepared to believe that one amongst us might be deceived by his senses or by his imagination, but it was clear that two persons could not see the same object from a different point of view and be simultaneously deluded by any effect of light or any optical hallucination.

'Each man was provided with a loaded revolver, a brandy and soda and a sufficient stock of pipes or cigars to last him through the night. We took up our position at eleven o'clock exactly, and waited.

'At first we were all four very silent and, as I have said before, slightly depressed; but as the hour wore away and nothing was seen or heard we began to talk to each other. Talking, however, was rather a difficulty. To begin with, we had to shout—at least we in the gallery had to shout to Henderson, down in the hall; and though Harford and Wells could converse quite comfortably, I, not being able to see the latter at all from my end of the gallery, had to pass my remarks to him second-hand through Harford, who amused himself in mis-stating every intelligent remark that I entrusted him with; added to which natural impediments to the 'flow of the soul,' the elements thought fit to create such a hullabaloo without that conversation was rendered still further work of difficulty.

'I never remember such a night in all my life. The rain came down in torrents; the wind howled and shrieked wildly amongst the tall chimneys and the bare elm trees without. Every now and then there was a lull, and then, again and again, a long sobbing moan came swirling round and round the house, for all the world like the cry of a human being in agony. It was a night to make one shudder, and thank Heaven for a roof over one's head.

'We all sat on at our separate posts hour after hour, listening to the wind and talking at intervals; but as the time wore on insensibly we became less and less talkative, and a sort of depression crept over us.

'At last we relapsed into a profound silence; then suddenly there came upon us all that chill blast of air, like a breath from a charnel-house, that we had experienced before, and almost simultaneously a hoarse cry broke from Henderson in the body of the hall below, and from Wells halfway up the stairs.

'Harford and I sprang to our feet, and we too saw it.

'The dead man was slowly coming up the stairs. He passed silently up with a sort of still, gliding motion, within a few inches of poor Wells, who shrank back, white with terror, against the wall. Henderson rushed wildly up the staircase in pursuit, whilst Harford and I, up on the gallery, fell instinctively back at his approach.

'He passed between us.

'We saw the glitter of his sightless eyes—the shrivelled skin upon his withered face—the mouth that fell away, like the mouth of a corpse, beneath his tawny beard. We felt the cold death-like blast that came with him, and the sickening horror of his terrible presence. Ah! can I ever forget it?'

With a strong shudder Jack Darent buried his face in his hands, and seemed too much overcome for some minutes to be able to proceed.

'My dear fellow, are you *sure,*' I said in an awestruck whisper.

He lifted his head.

'Forgive me, Lester; the whole business has shaken my nerves so thoroughly that I have not yet been able to get over it. But I have not yet told you the worst.'

'Good heavens—is there worse?' I ejaculated.

He nodded.

'No sooner,' he continued, 'had this awful creature passed us than Harford clutched at my arm and pointed to the farther end of the gallery

' "Look!" he cried hoarsely, "the nun!"

'There, coming towards us from the opposite direction, was the veiled figure of a nun.

'There were the long, flowing black and white garments—the gleam of the crucifix at her neck—the jangle of her rosary-beads from her waist; but her face was hidden.

'A sort of desperation seized me. With a violent effort over myself, I went towards this fresh apparition.

' "It *must* be a hoax," I said to myself, and there was a half-formed intention in my mind of wrenching aside the flowing draperies and of seeing for myself who and what it was. I strode towards the figure—I stood within half a yard of it. The nun raised her head slowly—and, Lester—*I saw her face!*

There was a moment's silence.

'What was it like, Jack?' I asked him presently.

He shook his head.

'That I can never tell to any living creature.'

'Was it so horrible?'

He nodded assent, shuddering.

'And what happened next?'

'I believe I fainted. At all events I remembered nothing further. They made me go to the vicarage the next day. I was so knocked over by it all—I was quite ill. I could not have stayed in the house. I stopped there all yesterday, and I got up to town this morning. I wish to Heaven I had taken your advice, old man, and had never gone to that horrible house.'

'I wish you had, Jack,' I answered fervently.

'Do you know that I shall die within the year?' he asked me presently.

I tried to pooh-pooh it.

'My dear fellow, don't take the thing so seriously as all that. Whatever may be the meaning of these horrible apparitions, there can be nothing but an old wife's fable in *that* saying. Why on earth should you die—you of all people, a great strong fellow with a constitution of iron? You don't look much like dying!'

'For all that I shall die. I cannot tell you why I am so certain—but I know that it will be so,' he answered in a low voice. 'And some terrible misfortune will happen to Harford—the other two never saw her—it is he and I who are doomed.'

⊠

A year has passed away. Last summer fashionable society rang for a week or more with the tale of poor Bob Harford's misfortune. The girl whom he was engaged to, and to whom he was devotedly attached—young, beautiful and wealthy—ran away on the eve of her wedding day with a drinking, swindling villain who had been turned out of ever so many clubs and tabooed for ages by every respectable man in town, and who had nothing but a handsome face and a fascinating manner to recommend him, and who by dint of these had succeeded in gaining a complete ascendancy over the fickle heart of poor Bob's lovely fiancee. As to Harford, he sold out and went off to the backwoods of Canada, and has never been heard of since.

And what of Jack Darent? Poor, handsome Jack, with his tall figure and his bright, happy face, and the merry blue eyes that had wiled Bella Lester's heart away! Alas! Far away in Southern Africa, poor Jack Darent lies in an unknown grave—slain by a Zulu assegai on the fatal plain of Isandula!

And Bella goes about clad in sable garments, heavy-eyed and stricken with sore grief. A widow in heart, if not in name.

The Hollow Man

By Thomas Burke

He came up one of the narrow streets which lead from the docks, and turned into a road whose farther end was gay with the light of London. At the end of this road he went deep into the lights of London, and sometimes into its shadows, farther and farther away from the river; and did not pause until he had reached a poor quarter near the centre.

He was a tall, spare figure, wearing a black mackintosh. Below this could be seen brown dungaree trousers. A peaked cap hid most of his face; the little that was exposed was white and sharp. In the autumn mist that filled the lighted streets as well as the dark he seemed a wraith, and some of those who passed him looked again, not sure whether they had indeed seen a living man. One or two of them moved their shoulders, as though shrinking from something.

His legs were long, but he walked with the short, deliberate steps of a blind man, though he was not blind. His eyes were open, and he stared straight ahead; but he seemed to see nothing and hear nothing.

Neither the mournful hooting of sirens across the black water of the river, nor the genial windows of the shops in the big streets near the centre drew his head to right or left. He walked as though he had no destination in mind, yet constantly, at this corner or that, he turned. It seemed that an unseen hand was guiding him to a given point of whose location he was himself ignorant.

He was searching for a friend of fifteen years ago, and the unseen hand, or some dog-instinct, had led him from Africa to London, and was now leading him, along the last mile of his search, to a certain little eating-house. He did not know that he was going to the eating- house of his friend Nameless, but he did know, from the time he left Africa, that he was journeying towards Nameless, and he now knew that he was very near to Nameless.

Nameless didn't know that his old friend was anywhere near though, had he observed conditions that evening, he might have wondered why he was sitting up an hour later than usual. He was seated in one of the pews of his prosperous little workmen's dining rooms—a little gold-mine his wife relations called it— and he was smoking and looking at nothing.

He had added up the till and written the copies of the bill of fare for next day, and there was nothing to keep him out of bed after his fifteen hours' attention to business. Had he been asked why he was sitting up later than usual, he would first have answered that he didn't know that he was, and would then have explained, in default of any other explanation, that it was for the purpose of having a last pipe. He was quite unaware that he was sitting up and keeping the door unlatched because a long-parted friend from Africa was seeking him and slowly approaching him, and needed his services.

He was quite unaware that he had left the door unlatched at that late hour—half-past eleven—to admit pain and woe.

But even as many bells sent dolefully across the night from their steeples their disagreement as to the point of half-past eleven, pain and woe were but two streets away from him. The mackintosh and dungarees and the sharp white face were coming nearer every moment.

There was silence in the house and in the streets; a heavy silence, broken, or sometimes stressed, by the occasional night-noises— motor horns, back-firing of lorries, shunting at a distant terminus. That silence seemed to envelop the house, but he did not notice it. He did not notice the bells, and he did not even notice the lagging step that approached his shop, and passed—and returned—and passed again—and halted. He was aware of nothing save that he was smoking a last pipe, and he was sitting in that state of hazy reverie which he called thinking, deaf and blind to anything not in his immediate neighbourhood.

But when a hand was laid on the latch, and the latch was lifted, he did hear that, and he looked up. And he saw the door open, he got up and went to it. And there, just within the door, he came face to face with the thin figure of pain and woe.

To kill a fellow-creature is a frightful thing. At the time the act is committed the murderer may have sound and convincing reasons (to him) for his act. But time and reflection may bring regret; even remorse; and this may live with him for many years. Examined in wakeful hours of the night or early morning, the reasons for the act may shed their cold logic, and may cease to be reasons and become mere excuses.

And these naked excuses may strip the murderer and show him to himself as he is. They may begin to hunt his soul, and to run into every little corner of his mind and every little nerve, in search of it.

And if to kill a fellow-creature and to suffer the recurrent regret for an act of heated blood is a frightful thing, it is still more frightful to kill a fellow-creature and bury his body deep in an African jungle, and then, fifteen years later, at about midnight, to see the latch of your door lifted by the hand you had stilled and to see the man, looking much as he did fifteen years ago, walk into your home and claim your hospitality.

⊠

When the man in mackintosh and dungarees walked into the dining rooms Nameless stood still; stared; staggered against a table; supported himself by a hand, and said, 'Oh!'

The other man said, 'Nameless!'

Then they looked at each other; Nameless with head thrust forward, mouth dropped; eyes wide; the visitor with a dull, glazed expression. If Nameless had not been the man he was—thick, bovine and costive—he would have flung up his arms and screamed. At that moment he felt the need of some such outlet, but did not know how to find it. The only dramatic expression he gave to the situation was to whisper instead of speak.

Twenty emotions came to life in his head and spine, and wrested there. But they showed themselves only in his staring eyes and his whisper. His first thought, or rather, spasm, was Ghosts-Indigestion Nervous-Breakdown. His second, when he saw that the figure was substantial and real, was Impersonation. But a slight movement of the part of the visitor dismissed that.

It was a little habitual movement which belonged only to that man; an unconscious twitching of the third finger of the left hand. He knew then that it was Gopak. Gopak, a little changed, but still, miraculously, thirty-two. Gopak, alive, breathing and real. No ghost. No phantom of the stomach. He was as certain of that as he was that fifteen years ago he had killed Gopak stone-dead and buried him.

The blackness of the moment was lightened by Gopak. In thin, flat tones he asked, 'May I sit down? I'm tired.' He sat down, and said, 'So tired. So tired.'

Nameless still held the table. He whispered: 'Gopak . . . Gopak . . . But I—I *killed* you. I killed you in the jungle. You were dead. I know you were.'

Gopak passed his hand across his face. He seemed about to cry. 'I know you did. I know. That's all I can remember—about this earth. You killed me.' The voice became thinner and flatter. 'And I was so comfortable. So comfortable. It was—such a rest. Such a rest as you don't know. And then they came and—disturbed me. They woke me up. And brought me back.' He sat with shoulders sagged, arms drooping, hands hanging between knees. After the first recognition he did not look at Nameless; he looked at the floor.

'Came and disturbed you?' Nameless leaned forward and whispered the words. 'Woke you up? Who?'

'The Leopard Men.'

'The what?'

'The Leopard Men.' The watery voice said it as casually as if it were saying 'the night watchman.'

'The Leopard Men?' Nameless stared, and his fat face crinkled in an effort to take in the situation of a midnight visitation from a dead man, and the dead man talking nonsense. He felt his blood moving out of its course. He looked at his own hand to see if it was his own hand. He looked at the table to see if it was his table. The hand and the table were facts, and if the dead man was a fact—and he was—his story might be a fact. It seemed anyway as sensible as the dead man's presence. He gave a heavy sigh from the stomach.

'A-ah... The Leopard Men... Yes, I heard about them out there. Tales!'

Gopak slowly wagged his head. 'Not tales. They're real. If they weren't real—I wouldn't be here. Would I? I'd be at rest.'

Nameless had to admit this. He had heard many tales 'out there' about the Leopard Men, and had dismissed them as jungle yarns. But now, it seemed, jungle yarns had become commonplace fact in a little London shop.

The watery voice went on. 'They do it. I saw them. I came back in the middle of a circle of them. They killed a nigger to put his life into me. They wanted a white man—for their farm. So they brought me back. You may not believe it. You wouldn't *want* to believe it. You wouldn't want to—see or know anything like them. And I wouldn't want any man to. But it's true. That's how I'm here.'

'But I left you absolutely dead. I made every test. It was three days before I buried you. And I buried you deep.'

'I know. But that wouldn't make any difference to them. It was a long time after when they came and brought me back. And I'm still dead, you know. It's only my body they brought back.' The voice trailed into a thread. 'And I'm so tired. So tired. I want to go back—to rest.' Sitting in his prosperous eating-house, Nameless was in the presence of an achieved miracle, but the everyday, solid appointments of the eating-house wouldn't let him fully comprehend it. Foolishly, as he realized when he had spoken, he asked Gopak to explain what had happened. Asked a man who couldn't really be alive to explain how he came to be alive. It was like asking Nothing to explain Everything.

Constantly, as he talked, he felt his grasp on his own mind slipping. The surprise of a sudden visitor at a late hour; the shock of the arrival of a long-dead man; and the realization that this long-dead man was not a wraith, were too much for him.

During the next half-hour he found himself talking to Gopak as to the Gopak he had known seventeen years ago when they were partners. Then he would be halted by the freezing knowledge that he was talking to a dead man, and that a dead man was faintly answering him. He felt that the thing couldn't really have happened, but in the interchange of talk he kept forgetting the improbable side of it, and accepting it. With each recollection of the truth, his mind would clear and settle in one thought—'I've got to get rid of him. How am I going to get rid of him?'

'But how did you get here?'

'I escaped.' The words came slowly and thinly, and out of the body rather than the mouth.

'How?'

'I don't—know. I don't remember anything—except our quarrel. And being at rest.'

'But why come all the way here? Why didn't you stay on the coast?'

'I don't—know. But you're the only man I know. The only man I can remember.'

'But how did you find me?'

'I don't know. But I had to—find you. You're the only man—who can help me.'

'But how can I help you?'

The head turned weakly from side to side. 'I don't—know. But nobody else—can.'

Nameless stared through the window, looking on to the lamplit street and seeing nothing of it. The everyday being which had been his half an hour ago had been annihilated; the everyday beliefs and disbeliefs shattered and mixed together. But some shred of his old sense and his old standard remained. He must handle this situation.

'Well—what you want to do? What you going to do? I don't see how I can help you. And you can't stay here, obviously.' A demon of perversity sent a facetious notion into his head—introducing Gopak to his wife—'This is my dead friend.'

But on his last spoken remark Gopak made the effort of raising his head and staring with the glazed eyes at Nameless. 'But I *must* stay here. There's nowhere else I can stay. I must stay here. That's why I came. You got to help me.'

'But you can't stay here. I got no room. All occupied. Nowhere for you to sleep.'

The wan voice said, 'That doesn't matter. I *can't* sleep.'

'Eh?'

'I *don't* sleep. I haven't slept since they brought me back. I can sit here—till you can think of some way of helping me.'

'But how *can* I?'

He again forgot the background of the situation, and began to get angry at the vision of a dead man sitting about the place waiting for him to think of something. 'How *can* I if you don't tell me how?'

'I don't—know. But you got to. You killed me. And I was dead—and comfortable. As it all came from you—killing me—you're responsible for me being—like this. So, you got to—help me. That's why I—came to you.'

'But what do you want me to do?'

'I don't—know. I can't—think. But nobody but you can help me. I had to come to you. Something brought me—straight to you. That means that you're the one—that can help me. Now I'm with you, something will—happen to help me. I feel it will. In time you'll—think of something.'

Nameless found his legs suddenly weak. He sat down and stared with a sick scowl at the hideous and the incomprehensible. Here was a dead man in his house—a man he had murdered in a moment of black temper—and he knew in his heart that he couldn't turn the man out. For one thing, he would have been afraid to touch him; he couldn't see himself touching him. For another, faced with the miracle of the presence of a fifteen-years-dead man, he doubted whether physical force or any material agency would be effectual in moving the man.

His soul shivered, as all men's souls shiver at the demonstration of forces outside their mental or spiritual horizon. He had murdered this man, and often, in fifteen years, he had repented the act. If the man's appalling story were true, then he had some sort of right to turn to Nameless. Nameless recognized that, and knew that whatever happened he couldn't turn him out. His hot-tempered sin had literally come home to him.

The wan voice broke into his nightmare. 'You go to rest, Nameless. I'll sit here. You go to rest.' He put his face down to his hands and uttered a little moan. 'Oh, why can't I rest? Why can't I go back to my beautiful rest?'

⊠

Nameless came down early next morning with a half-hope that Gopak would not be there. But he was there, seated where Nameless had left him last night. Nameless made some tea, and showed him where he might wash. He washed listlessly, and crawled back to his seat, and listlessly drank the tea which Nameless brought to him.

To his wife and the kitchen helpers Nameless mentioned him as an old friend who had had a bit of a shock. 'Shipwrecked and knocked on the head. But quite harmless, and he won't be staying long. He's waiting for admission to a home. A good pal to me in the past, and it's the least I can do to let him stay here a few days. Suffers from sleeplessness and prefers to sit up at night. Quite harmless.'

But Gopak stayed more than a few days. He outstayed everybody. Even when the customers had gone Gopak was still there.

On the first morning of his visit when the regular customers came in at midday, they looked at the odd, white figure sitting vacantly in the first pew, then stared, then moved away.

All avoided the pew in which he sat. Nameless explained him to them, but his explanation did not seem to relieve the slight tension which settled on the dining room. The atmosphere was not so brisk and chatty as usual. Even those who had their backs to the stranger seemed to be affected by his presence.

At the end of the first day Nameless, noticing this, told him that he had arranged a nice corner of the front room upstairs, where he could sit by the window and took his arm to take him upstairs. But Gopak feebly shook the hand away, and sat where he was. 'No. I don't want to go. I'll stay here. I'll stay here. I don't want to move.'

And he wouldn't move. After a few more pleadings Nameless realized with dismay that his refusal was definite; that it would be futile to press him or force him; that he was going to sit in that dining room for ever. He was as weak as a child and as firm as a rock.

He continued to sit in that first pew, and the customers continued to avoid it, and to give queer glances at it. It seemed that they half recognized that he was something more than a fellow who had had a shock.

During the second week of his stay three of the regular customers were missing, and more than one of those that remained made acidly facetious suggestions to Nameless that he park his lively friend somewhere else. He made things too exciting for them; all that whoopee took them off their work, and interfered with digestion. Nameless told them he would be staying only a day or so longer; but they found that this was untrue, and at the end of the second week eight of the regulars had found another place.

Each day, when the dinner hour came, Nameless tried to get him to take a little walk, but always he refused.

He would go out only at night, and then never more than two hundred yards from the shop. For the rest, he sat in his pew, sometimes dozing in the afternoon, at other times staring at the floor. He took his food abstractedly, and never knew whether he had had food or not. He spoke only when questioned, and the burden of his talk was 'I'm so tired. So tired.'

One thing only seemed to arouse any light of interest in him; one thing only drew his eyes from the floor. That was the seventeen-year- old daughter of his host, who was known as Bubbles, and who helped with the waiting. And Bubbles seemed to be the only member of the shop and its customers who did not shrink from him.

She knew nothing of the truth about him, but she seemed to understand him, and the only response he ever gave to anything was to her childish sympathy. She sat and chatted foolish chatter to him—'bringing him out of himself' she called it—and sometimes he would be brought out to the extent of a watery smile. He came to recognize her step, and would look up before she entered the room. Once or twice in the evening, when the shop was empty, and Nameless was sitting miserably with him, he would ask, without lifting his eyes. 'Where's Bubbles?' and would be told that Bubbles had gone to the pictures or was out at a dance, and would relapse into deeper vacancy.

Nameless didn't like this. He was already visited by a curse which, in four weeks, had destroyed most of his business. Regular customers had dropped off two by two, and no new customers came to take their place. Strangers who dropped in once for a meal did not come again; they could not keep their eyes or their minds off the forbidding, white-faced figure sitting motionless in the first pew. At midday, when the place had been crowded and late-comers had to wait for a seat, it was now two-thirds empty; only a few of the most thick-skinned remained faithful.

And on top of this there was the interest of the dead man in his daughter, an interest which seemed to be having an unpleasant effect. Nameless hadn't noticed it, but his wife had. 'Bubbles don't seem as bright and lively as she was. You noticed it lately? She's getting quiet—and a bit slack. Sits about a lot. Paler than she used to be.'

'Her age, perhaps.'

'No, She's not one of these thin dark sort. No—it's something else. Just the last week or two I've noticed it. Off her food. Sits about doing nothing. No interest. May be nothing; just out of sorts, perhaps... How much longer's that horrible friend of yours going to stay?'

⊠

The horrible friend stayed some weeks longer—ten weeks in all—while Nameless watched his business drop to nothing and his daughter get pale and peevish. He knew the cause of it. There was no home in all England like his: no home that had a dead man sitting in it for ten weeks. A dead man brought, after a long time, from the grave, to sit and disturb his customers and take the vitality from his daughter. He couldn't tell this to anybody. Nobody would believe such nonsense.

But he *knew* that he was entertaining a dead man, and, knowing that a long-dead man was walking the earth, he could believe in any result of that fact. He could believe almost anything that he would have derided ten weeks ago. His customers had abandoned his shop, not because of the presence of a silent, white-faced man, but because of the presence of a dead-living man.

Their minds might not know it, but their blood knew it. And, as his business had been destroyed, so, he believed, would his daughter be destroyed. Her blood was not warming her; her blood told her only that this was a long-ago friend of her father's, and she was drawn to him.

It was at this point that Nameless, having no work to do, began to drink. And it was well that he did so. For out of the drink came an idea, and with that idea he freed himself from the curse upon him and his house.

The shop now served scarcely half a dozen customers at midday. It had become ill-kempt and dusty, and the service and the food were bad. Nameless took no trouble to be civil to his few customers. Often, when he was notably under drink, he went to the trouble of being very rude to them. They talked about this. They talked about the decline of his business and the dustiness of the shop and the bad food. They talked about his drinking, and, of course, exaggerated it.

And they talked about the queer fellow who sat there day after day and gave everybody the creeps. A few outsiders, hearing the gossip, came to the dining rooms to see the queer fellow and the always-tight proprietor; but they did not come again, and there were not enough of the curious to keep the place busy. It went down until it served scarcely two customers a day. And Nameless went down with it into drink.

Then, one evening, out of the drink he fished an inspiration.

He took it downstairs to Gopak, who was sitting in his usual seat, hands hanging, eyes on the floor. 'Gopak—listen. You came here because I was the only man who could help you in your trouble. You listening?'

A faint 'Yes' was his answer.

'Well, now. You told me I'd got to think of something. I've thought of something. . . Listen. You say I'm responsible for your condition and got to get you out of it, because I killed you. I did. We had a row. You made me wild. You dared me. And what with that sun and the jungle and the insects, I wasn't myself. I killed you. The moment it was done I could a-cut me right hand off. Because you and me were pals. I could a-cut me right hand off.'

'I know. I felt that directly it was over. I knew you were suffering.'

'Ah!. . . I have suffered. And I'm suffering now. Well, this is what I've thought. All your present trouble comes from me killing you in that jungle and burying you. An idea came to me. Do you think it would help you—do you think it would put you back to rest if I—if I—if I—killed you again?'

For some seconds Gopak continued to stare at the floor. Then his shoulders moved. Then, while Nameless watched every little response to his idea, the Watery voice began. 'Yes. Yes. That's it. That's what I was waiting for. That's why I came here. I can see now. That's why I had to get here. Nobody else could kill me. Only you. I've got to be killed again. Yes, I see. But nobody else—would be able—to kill me. Only the man who first killed me... Yes, you've found—what we're both—waiting for. Anybody else could shoot me—stab me—hang me—but they couldn't kill me. Only you. That's why I managed to get here and find you.'

The watery voice rose to a thin strength. 'That's it. And you must do it. Do it now. You don't want to, I know. But you must. You *must.*'

His head drooped and he stared at the floor. Nameless, too, stared at the floor. He was seeing things. He had murdered a man and had escaped all punishment save that of his own mind, which had been terrible enough. But now he was going to murder him again—not in a jungle but in a city; and he saw the slow points of the result.

He saw the arrest. He saw the first hearing. He saw the trial. He saw the cell. He saw the rope. He shuddered.

Then he saw the alternative—the breakdown of his life—a ruined business, poverty, the poorhouse, a daughter robbed of her health and perhaps dying, and always the curse of the dead-living man, who might follow him to the poorhouse. Better to end it all, he thought. Rid himself of the curse which Gopak had brought upon him and his family, and then rid his family of himself with a revolver. Better to follow up his idea.

He got stiffly to his feet. The hour was late evening—half-past ten—and the streets were quiet. He had pulled down the shop-blinds and locked the door. The room was lit by one light at the further end. He moved about uncertainly and looked at Gopak. 'Er—how would you—how shall I——'

Gopak said, 'You did it with a knife. Just under the heart. You must do it that way again.'

Nameless stood and looked at him for some seconds. Then, with an air of resolve, he shook himself. He walked quickly to the kitchen.

Three minutes later his wife and daughter heard a crash, as though a table had been overturned. They called but got no answer. When they came down they found him sitting in one of the pews, wiping sweat from his forehead. He was white and shaking, and appeared to be recovering from a faint.

'Whatever's the matter? You all right?'

He waved them away. 'Yes, I'm all right. Touch of giddiness. Smoking too much, I think.'

'Mmmm. Or drinking... Where's your friend? Out for a walk?'

'No. He's gone off. Said he wouldn't impose any longer, and'd go and find an infirmary.' He spoke weakly and found trouble in

picking words. 'Didn't you hear that bang—when he shut the door?'
'I thought that was you fell down.'

'No. It was him when he went. I couldn't stop him.'

'Mmmm. Just as well, I think.' She looked about her. 'Things seem to a-gone wrong since he's been here.'

There was a general air of dustiness about the place. The table- cloths were dirty, not from use but from disuse. The windows were dim. A long knife, very dusty, was lying on the table under the window. In a corner by the door leading to the kitchen, unseen by her, lay a dusty mackintosh and dungaree, which appeared to have been tossed there. But it was over by the main door, near the first pew, that the dust was thickest—a long trail of it—greyish-white dust.

'Really this place gets more and more slapdash. Why can't you attend to business? You didn't use to be like this. No wonder it's gone down, letting the place get into this state. Why don't you pull yourself together. Just *look* at that dust by the door. Looks as though somebody's been spilling ashes all over the place.'

Nameless looked at it, and his hands shook a little. But he answered, more firmly than before: 'Yes, I know. I'll have a proper clean-up tomorrow. I'll put it all to rights tomorrow. I been getting a bit slack.'

For the first time in ten weeks he smiled at them; a thin, haggard smile, but a smile.

The Thing in the Upper Room

By Arthur Morrison

A shadow hung ever over the door, which stood black in the depth of its arched recess, like an unfathomable eye under a frowning brow. The landing was wide and panelled, and a heavy rail, supported by a carved balustrade, stretched away in alternate slopes and levels down the dark staircase, past other doors, and so to the courtyard and the street. The other doors were dark also; but it was with a difference. That top landing was lightest of all, because of the skylight; and perhaps it was largely by reason of contrast that its one doorway gloomed so black and forbidding. The doors below opened and shut, slammed, stood ajar. Men and women passed in and out, with talk and human sounds—sometimes even with laughter or a snatch of song; but the door on the top landing remained shut and silent through weeks and months. For, in truth, the *lodgement* had an ill name, and had been untenanted for years. Long even before the last tenant had occupied it, the room had been regarded with fear and aversion, and the end of that last tenant had in no way lightened the gloom that hung about the place.

The house was so old that its weather-washed face may well have looked down on the bloodshed of St. Bartholomew's, and the haunted room may even have earned its ill name on that same day of death. But Paris is a city of cruel history, and since the old mansion rose proud and new, the *hotel* of some powerful noble, almost any year of the centuries might have seen the blot fall on that upper room that had left it a place of loathing and shadows. The occasion was long forgotten, but the fact remained; whether or not some horror of the *ancient regime* or some enormity of the Terror was enacted in that room was no longer to be discovered; but nobody would live there, nor stay beyond that gloomy door one second longer than he could help. It might be supposed that the fate of the solitary tenant within living memory had something to do with the matter—and, indeed, his end was sinister enough; but long before his time the room had stood shunned and empty. He, greatly daring, had taken no more heed of the common terror of the room than to use it to his advantage in abating the rent; and he had shot himself a little later, while the police were beating at his door to arrest him on a charge of murder. As I have said, his fate may have added to the general aversion from the place, though it had in no way originated it; and now ten years had passed, and more, since his few articles of furniture had been carried away and sold; and nothing had been carried in to replace them.

When one is twenty-five, healthy, hungry and poor, one is less likely to be frightened from a cheap lodging by mere headshakings than might be expected in other circumstances. Attwater was twenty-five, commonly healthy, often hungry, and always poor. He came to live in Paris because, from his remembrance of his student days, he believed he could live cheaper there than in London; while it was quite certain that he would not sell fewer pictures, since he had never yet sold one.

It was the *concierge* of a neighbouring house who showed Attwater the room. The house of the room itself maintained no such functionary, though its main door stood open day and night. The man said little, but his surprise at Attwater's application was plain to see. Monsieur was English? Yes. The *logement* was convenient, though high, and probably now a little dirty, since it had not been occupied recently. Plainly, the man felt it to be no business of his to enlighten an unsuspecting foreigner as to the reputation of the place; and if he could let it there would be some small gratification from the landlord, though, at such a rent, of course a very small one indeed.

But Attwater was better informed than the *concierge* supposed. He had heard the tale of the haunted room, vaguely and incoherently, it is true, from the little old engraver of watches on the floor below, by whom he had been directed to the *concierge*. The old man had been voluble and friendly, and reported that the room had a good light, facing northeast—indeed, a much better light than he, engraver of watches, enjoyed on the floor below. So much so that, considering this advantage and the much lower rent, he himself would have taken the room long ago, except—well, except for other things. Monsieur was a stranger, and perhaps had no fear to inhabit a haunted chamber; but that was its reputation, as everybody in the quarter knew; it would be a misfortune, however, to a stranger to take the room without suspicion, and to undergo unexpected experiences. Here, however, the old man checked himself, possibly reflecting that too much information to inquirers after the upper room might offend his landlord. He hinted as much, in fact, hoping that his friendly warning would not be allowed to travel farther. As to the precise nature of the disagreeable manifestations in the room, who could say? Perhaps there were really none at all. People said this and that. Certainly, the place had been untenanted for many years, and he would not like to stay in it himself. But it might be the good fortune of monsieur to break the spell, and if monsieur was resolved to defy the *revenant,* he wished monsieur the highest success and happiness.

So much for the engraver of watches; and now the *concierge* of the neighbouring house led the way up the stately old panelled staircase, swinging his keys in his hand, and halted at last before the dark door in the frowning recess. He turned the key with some difficulty, pushed open the door, and stood back with an action of something not wholly deference, to allow Attwater to enter first.

A sort of small lobby had been partitioned off at some time, though except for this the *logement* was of one large room only. There was something unpleasant in the air of the place—not a smell, when one came to analyze one's sensations, though at first it might seem so. Attwater walked across to the wide window and threw it open. The chimneys and roofs of many houses of all ages straggled before him, and out of the welter rose the twin towers of St. Sulpice, scarred and grim.

Air the room as one might, it was unpleasant; a sickly, even a cowed, feeling, invaded one through all the senses—or perhaps through none of them. The feeling was there, though it was not easy to say by what channel it penetrated. Attwater was resolved to admit none but a commonsense explanation, and blamed the long closing of door and window; and the *concierge,* standing uneasily near the door, agreed that that must be it. For a moment Attwater wavered, despite himself. But the rent was very low, and, low as it was, he could not afford a sou more. The light was good, though it was not a top-light, and the place was big enough for his simple requirements. Attwater reflected that he should despise himself ever after if he shrank from the opportunity, it would be one of those secret humiliations that will rise again and again in a man's memory, and make him blush in solitude. He told the *concierge* to leave door and window wide open for the rest of the day, and he clinched the bargain.

It was with something of amused bravado that he reported to his few friends in Paris his acquisition of a haunted room; for, once out of the place, he readily convinced himself that his disgust and dislike while in the room were the result of imagination and nothing more. Certainly there was no rational reason to account for the unpleasantness; consequently, what could it be but a matter of fancy? He resolved to face the matter from the beginning, and clear his mind from any foolish prejudices that the hints of the old engraver might have inspired, by forcing himself through whatever adventures he might encounter. In fact, as he walked the streets about his business, and arranged for the purchase and delivery of the few simple articles of furniture that would be necessary, his enterprise assumed the guise of a pleasing adventure. He remembered that he had made an attempt, only a year or two ago, to spend a night in a house reputed haunted in England, but had failed to find the landlord. Here was the adventure to hand, with promise of a tale to tell in future times; and a welcome idea struck him that he might look out the ancient history of the room, and work the whole thing into a magazine article, which would bring a little money.

So simple were his needs that by the afternoon of the day following his first examination of the room it was ready for use.

He took his bag from the cheap hotel in a little street of Montparnasse, where he had been lodging, and carried it to his new home. The key was now in his pocket, and for the first time he entered the place alone. The window remained wide open but it was still there—that depressing, choking something that entered the consciousness he knew not by what gate. Again he accused his fancy. He stamped and whistled, and set about unpacking a few canvases and a case of old oriental weapons that were part of his professional properties. But he could give no proper attention to the work, and detected himself more than once yielding to a childish impulse to look over his shoulder. He laughed at himself— with some effort—and sat determinedly to smoke a pipe, and grow used to his surroundings. But presently he found himself, pushing his chair farther and farther back, till it touched the wall. He would take the whole room into view, he said to himself in excuse, and stare it out of countenance. So he sat and smoked, and as he sat his eye fell on a Malay dagger that lay on the table between him and the window. It was a murderous, twisted thing, and its pommel was fashioned into the semblance of a bird's head, with curved beak and an eye of some dull red stone. He found himself gazing on this red eye with an odd, mindless fascination. The dagger in its wicked curves seemed now a creature of some outlandish fantasy—a snake with a beaked head, a thing of nightmare, in some new way dominant, overruling the centre of his perceptions. The rest of the room grew dim, but the red stone glowed with a fuller light; nothing more was present to his consciousness. Then, with a sudden clang, the heavy bell of St. Sulpice aroused him, and he started up in some surprise.

There lay the dagger on the table, strange and murderous enough, but merely as he had always known it. He observed with more surprise, however, that his chair, which had been back against the wall, was now some six feet forward, close by the table; clearly he must have drawn it forward in his abstraction, towards the dagger on which his eyes had been fixed. . . The great bell of St. Sulpice went clanging on, repeating its monotonous call to the Angelus.

He was cold, almost shivering. He flung the dagger into a drawer, and turned to go out. He saw by his watch that it was later than he had supposed; his fit of abstraction must have lasted some time. Perhaps he had even been dozing.

He went slowly downstairs and out into the streets. As he went he grew more and more ashamed of himself, for he had to confess that in some inexplicable way he feared that room. He had seen nothing, heard nothing of the kind that one might have expected, or had heard of in any room reputed haunted; he could not help thinking that it would have been some sort of relief if he had. But there was an all-pervading, overpowering sense of another Presence—something abhorrent, not human, something almost physically nauseous. Withal it was something more than presence; it was power, domination—so he seemed to remember it. And yet the remembrance grew weaker as he walked in the gathering dusk; he thought of a story he had once read of a haunted house wherein it was shown that the house actually was haunted by the spirit of fear, and nothing else. That, he persuaded himself, was the case with his room; he felt angry at the growing conviction that he had allowed himself to be overborne by fancy—by the spirit of fear.

He returned that night with the resolve to allow himself no foolish indulgence. He had heard nothing and had seen nothing; when something palpable to the senses occurred, it would be time enough to deal with it. He took off his clothes and got into bed deliberately leaving candle and matches at hand in case of need. He had expected to find some difficulty in sleeping, or at least some delay but he was scarce well in bed ere he fell into a heavy sleep.

Dazzling sunlight through the window woke him in the morning, and he sat up, staring sleepily about him. He must have slept like a log. But he had been dreaming; the dreams were horrible. His head ached beyond anything he had experienced before, and he was far more tired than when he went to bed. He sank back on he pillow, but the mere contact made his head ring with pain. He got out of bed, and found himself staggering; it was all as though he had been drunk—unspeakably drunk with bad liquor. His dreams—they had been horrid dreams; he could remember that they had been bad, but what they actually were was now gone from him entirely. He rubbed his eyes and stared amazedly down at the table: where the crooked dagger lay, with its bird's head and red stone eye. It lay just as it had lain when he sat gazing at it yesterday, and yet he would have sworn that he had flung that same dagger into a drawer. Perhaps he had dreamed it; at any rate, he put the thing carefully into the drawer now, and, still with his ringing headache, dressed himself and went out.

As he reached the next landing the old engraver greeted him from his door with an inquiring good-day. 'Monsieur has not slept: well, I fear?'

In some doubt, Attwater protested that he had slept quite soundly. 'And as yet I have neither seen nor heard anything of the ghost,' he added.

'Nothing?' replied the old man, with a lift of the eyebrows, 'nothing at all? It is fortunate. It seemed to me, here below, that monsieur was moving about very restlessly in the night; but no doubt I was mistaken. No doubt, also, I may felicitate monsieur on breaking the evil tradition. We shall hear no more of it; monsieur has the good fortune of a brave heart.'

He smiled and bowed pleasantly, but it was with something of a puzzled look that his eyes followed Attwater descending the staircase.

Attwater took his coffee and roll after an hour's walk, and fell asleep in his seat. Not for long, however, and presently he rose and left the cafe. He felt better, though still unaccountably fatigued. He caught sight of his face in a mirror beside a shop window, and saw an improvement since he had looked in his own glass. That indeed had brought him a shock. Worn and drawn beyond what might have been expected of so bad a night, there was even something more. What was it? How should it remind him of that old legend—was it Japanese?—which he had tried to recollect when he had wondered confusedly at the haggard apparition that confronted him? Some tale of a demon-possessed person who in any mirror, saw never his own face, but the face of the demon.

Work he felt to be impossible, and he spent the day on garden seats, at cafe tables, and for a while in the Luxembourg. And in the evening he met an English friend, who took him by the shoulders and looked into his eyes, shook him, and declared that he had been overworking, and needed, above all things, a good dinner, which he should have instantly. 'You'll dine with me,' he said, 'at La Perouse, and we'll get a cab to take us there. I'm hungry.'

As they stood and looked for a passing cab a man ran shouting with newspapers. 'We'll have a cab,' Attwater's friend repeated, 'and we'll take the new murder with us for conversation's sake. Hi! *Journal!'*

He bought a paper, and followed Attwater into the cab. 'I've a strong idea I knew the poor old boy by sight,' he said. 'I believe he'd seen better days.'

'Who?'

'The old man who was murdered in the Rue Broca last night. The description fits exactly. He used to hang about the cafes and run messages. It isn't easy to read in this cab; but there's probably nothing fresh in this edition. They haven't caught the murderer, anyhow.'

Attwater took the paper, and struggled to read it in the changing light. A poor old man had been found dead on the footpath of the Rue Broca, torn with a score of stabs. He had been identified —an old man not known to have a friend in the world; also, because he was so old and so poor, probably not an enemy. There was no robbery; the few sous the old man possessed remained in his pocket. He must have been attacked on his way home in the early hours of the morning, possibly by a homicidal maniac, and stabbed again and again with inconceivable fury. No arrest had been made.

Attwater pushed the paper away: 'Pah!' he said; 'I don't like it. I'm a bit off colour and I was dreaming horribly all last night; though why this should remind me of it I can't guess. But it's no cure for the blues, this!'

'No,' replied his friend heartily; 'we'll get that upstairs, for here we are, on the quay. A bottle of the best Burgundy on the list and the best dinner they can do—that's your physic. Come!'

It was a good prescription, indeed. Attwater's friend was cheerful and assiduous, and nothing could have bettered the dinner. Attwater found himself reflecting that indulgence in the blues was a poor pastime, with no better excuse than a bad night's rest. And last night's dinner in comparison with this! Well, it was enough to have spoiled his sleep, that one-franc-fifty dinner.

Attwater left La Perouse as gay as his friend. They had sat late, and now there was nothing to do but cross the water and walk a little in the boulevards. This they did, and finished the evening at a cafe table with half a dozen acquaintances.

Attwater walked home with a light step, feeling less drowsy than at any time during the day. He was well enough. He felt he should soon get used to the room. He had been a little too much alone lately, and that had got on his nerves. It was simply stupid.

Again he slept quickly and heavily—and dreamed. But he had an awakening of another sort. No bright sun blazed in at the open window to lift his heavy lids, and no morning bell from St. Sulpice opened his ears to the cheerful noise of the city. He awoke gasping and staring in the dark, rolling face-downward on the floor, catching his breath in agonized sobs; while through the window from the streets came a clamour of hoarse cries: cries of pursuit and the noise of running men: a shouting and clatter wherein here and their a voice was clear among the rest—'Al'assassin! Arretez!'

He dragged himself to his feet in the dark, gasping still. What was this—all this? Again a dream? His legs trembled under him, and he sweated with fear. He made for the window, panting and feeble; and then, as he supported himself by the sill, he realized wonderingly that he was fully dressed—that he wore even his hat. The running crowd straggled through the outer street and away, the shouts growing fainter. What had wakened him? Why had he dressed? He remembered his matches, and turned to grope for them; but something was already in his hand—something wet, sticky. He dropped it on the table, and even as he struck the light, before he saw it, he knew. The match sputtered and flared, and there on the table lay the crooked dagger, smeared and dripping and horrible.

Blood was on his hands—the match stuck in his fingers. Caught at the heart by the first grip of an awful surmise, he looked up and saw in the mirror before him, in the last flare of the match, the face of the Thing in the Room.

The Monkey's Paw

By W.W. Jacobs

Without, the night was cold and wet, but in the small parlour of Laburnam Villa the blinds were drawn and the fire burned brightly. Father and son were at chess, the former, who possessed ideas about the game involving radical changes, putting his king into such sharp and unnecessary perils that it even provoked comment from the white-haired old lady knitting placidly by the fire.

'Hark at the wind,' said Mr White, who, having seen a fatal mistake after it was too late, was amiably desirous of preventing his son from seeing it.

'I'm listening,' said the latter, grimly surveying the board as he stretched out his hand. 'Check.'

'I should hardly think that he'd come tonight,' said his father, with his hand poised over the board.

'Mate,' replied the son.

'That's the worst of living so far out,' bawled Mr White, with sudden and unlooked for violence; 'of all the beastly, slushy, out-of-the-way places to live in, this is the worst. Pathway's a bog, and the road's a torrent. I don't know what people are thinking about. I suppose because only two houses in the road are let, they think it doesn't matter.'

'Never mind, dear,' said his wife, soothingly; 'perhaps you'll win the next one.'

Mr White looked up sharply, just in time to intercept a knowing glance between mother and son. The words died away on his lips, and he hid a guilty grin in his thin grey beard.

'There he is,' said Herbert White, as the gate banged to loudly and heavy footsteps came toward the door.

The old man rose with hospitable haste, and opening the door, was heard condoling with the new arrival. The new arrival also condoled with himself, so that Mrs White said, 'Tut, tut!' and coughed gently as her husband entered the room, followed by a tall, burly man, beady of eye and rubicund of visage.

'Sergeant-Major Morris,' he said, introducing him.

The sergeant-major shook hands, and taking the proffered seat by the fire, watched contentedly while his host got out whisky and tumblers and stood a small copper kettle on the fire.

At the third glass his eyes got brighter, and he began to talk, the 'little family circle regarding with eager interest this visitor from distant parts, as he squared his broad shoulders in the chair and spoke of wild scenes and doughty deeds; of wars and plagues and strange peoples.

'Twenty-one years of it,' said Mr, White, nodding at his wife and son. 'When he went away he was a slip of a youth in the warehouse. Now look at him.'

'He don't look to have taken much harm,' said Mrs White, politely.

'I'd like to go to India myself,' said the old man, 'just to look round a bit, you know.'

'Better where you are,' said the sergeant-major, shaking his head. He put down the empty glass, and sighing softly, shook it again.

'I should like to see those old temples and fakirs and jugglers,' said the old man. 'What was that you started telling me the other day about a monkey's paw or something, Morris?'

'Nothing,' said the soldier, hastily, 'Leastways nothing worth hearing.'

'Monkey's paw?' said Mrs White, curiously.

'Well, it's just a bit of what you might call magic, perhaps,' said the sergeant-major, off-handedly.

His three listeners leaned forward eagerly. The visitor-absent-mindedly put his empty glass to his lips and then set it down again. His host filled it for him.

'To look at,' said the sergeant-major, fumbling in his pocket, 'it's just an ordinary little paw, dried to a mummy.'

He took something out of his pocket and proffered it. Mrs White drew back with a grimace, but her son, taking it, examined it curiously.

'And what is there special about it?' inquired Mr White as he took it from his son, and having examined it, placed it upon the table.

'It had a spell put on it by an old fakir,' said the sergeant-major, 'a very holy man. He wanted to show that fate ruled people's lives, and that those who interfered with it did so to their sorrow. He put a spell on it so that three separate men could each have three wishes from it.'

His manner was so impressive that his hearers were conscious that their light laughter jarred somewhat.

'Well, why don't you have three, sir?' said Herbert White, cleverly.

The soldier regarded him in the way that middle age is wont to regard presumptuous youth. 'I have,' he said, quietly, and his blotchy face whitened.

'And did you really have the three wishes granted?' asked Mrs White. 'I did,' said the sergeant-major, and his glass tapped against his strong teeth.

'And has anybody else wished?' persisted the old lady.

'The first man had his three wishes. Yes,' was the reply; 'I don't know what the first two were, but the third was for death. That's how I got the paw.'

His tones were so grave that a hush fell upon the group.

'If you've had your three wishes, it's no good to you now, then, Morris,' said the old man at last. 'What do you keep it for?'

The soldier shook his head. 'Fancy, I suppose,' he said, slowly. 'I did have some idea of selling it, but I don't think I will. It has caused enough mischief already. Besides, people won't buy. They think it's a fairy tale; some of them, and those who do think anything of it want to try it first and pay me afterward.'

'If you could have another three wishes,' said the old man, eyeing him keenly, 'would you have them?'

'I don't know,' said the other. 'I don't know.'

He took the paw, and dangling it between his forefinger and thumb, suddenly threw it upon the fire. White, with a slight cry, stooped down and snatched it off.

'Better let it burn,' said the soldier, solemnly.

'If you don't want it, Morris,' said the other, 'give it to me.'

'I won't,' said his friend, doggedly. 'I threw it on the fire. If you keep it, don't blame me for what happens. Pitch it on the fire again like a sensible man.'

The other shook his head and examined his new possession closely. 'How do you do it?' he inquired.

'Hold it up in your right hand and wish aloud,' said the sergeant-major, 'but I warn you of the consequences.'

Sounds like the *Arabian Nights*' said Mrs White, as she rose and began to set the supper. 'Don't you think you might wish for four pairs of hands for me?'

Her husband drew the talisman from pocket, and then all three burst into laughter as the sergeant-major, with a look of alarm on his face, caught him by the arm.

'If you must wish,' he said, gruffly, 'wish for something sensible.'

Mr White dropped it back in his pocket, and placing chairs, motioned his friend to the table. In the business of supper the talisman was partly forgotten, and afterward the three sat listening in an enthralled fashion to a second instalment of the soldier's adventures in India.

'If the tale about the monkey's paw is not more truthful than those he has been telling us,' said Herbert, as the door closed behind their guest, just in time for him to catch the last train, 'we shan't make much out of it.'

'Did you give him anything for it, father?' inquired Mrs White, regarding her husband closely.

'A trifle,' said he, colouring slightly. 'He didn't want it, but I made him take it. And he pressed me again to throw it away.'

'Likely,' said Herbert, with pretended horror. 'Why, we're going to be rich, and famous and happy. Wish to be an emperor, father, to begin with; then you can't be henpecked.'

He darted round the table, pursued by the maligned Mrs White armed with an antimacassar.

Mr White took the paw from his pocket and eyed it dubiously 1 don't know what to wish for, and that's a fact,' he said, slowly 'It seems to me I've got all I want.'

'If you only cleared the house, you'd be quite happy, wouldn't you?' said Herbert, with his hand on his shoulder. 'Well, wish for two hundred pounds, then; that'll just do it.'

His father, smiling shamefacedly at his own credulity, held up the talisman, as his son, with a solemn face, somewhat marred by a wink at his mother, sat down at the piano and struck a few impressive chords.

'I wish for two hundred pounds,' said the old man distinctly. A fine crash from the piano greeted the words, interrupted by a shuddering cry from the old man. His wife and son ran toward him.

'It moved,' he cried, with a glance of disgust at the object as it lay on the floor. As I wished, it twisted in my hand like a snake.'

'Well, I don't see the money,' said his son as he picked it up and placed it on the table, 'and I bet I never shall.'

'It must have been your fancy, father,' said his wife, regarding him anxiously.

He shook his head. 'Never mind, though; there's no harm done, but it gave me a shock all the same.'

They sat down by the fire again while the two men finished their pipes. Outside, the wind was higher than ever, and the old man started nervously at the sound of a door banging upstairs. A silence unusual and depressing settled upon all three, which lasted until the old couple rose to retire for the night.

'I expect you'll find the cash tied up in a big bag in the middle of your bed,' said Herbert, as he bade them goodnight, 'and something horrible squatting up on top of the wardrobe washing you pocket your ill-gotten gains.'

He sat alone in the darkness, gazing at the dying fire, and seeing faces in it. The last face was so horrible and so simian that he gazed at it in amazement. It got so vivid that, with a little uneasy laugh, he felt on the table for a glass containing a little water to throw over it. His hand grasped the monkey's paw, and with a little shiver he wiped his hand on his coat and went up to bed.

II

In the brightness of the wintry sun next morning as it streamed over the breakfast table he laughed at his fears. There was an air of prosaic wholesomeness about the room which it had lacked on the previous night, and the dirty, shrivelled little paw was pitched on the sideboard with a carelessness which betokened no great belief in its virtues.

'I suppose all old soldiers are the same,' said Mrs White. 'The idea of our listening to such nonsense! How could wishes be granted in these days? And if they could, how could two hundred pounds hurt you, father?'

'Might drop on his head from the sky,' said the frivolous Herbert.

'Morris said the things happened so naturally,' said his father, 'that you might if you so wished attribute it to coincidence.'

'Well, don't break into the money before I come back,' said Herbert as he rose from the table. 'I'm afraid it'll turn you into a mean, avaricious man, and we shall have to disown you.'

His mother laughed, and following him to the door, watched him down the road; and returning to the breakfast table, was very happy at the expense of her husband's credulity. All of which did not prevent her from scurrying to the door at the postman's knock, nor prevent her from referring somewhat shortly to retired sergeant-majors of bibulous habits when she found that the post brought a tailor's bill.

'Herbert will have some more of his funny remarks, I expect, when he comes home,' she said, as they sat at dinner.

'I dare say,' said Mr White, pouring himself out some beer; 'but for all that, the thing moved in my hand; that I'll swear to.'

'You thought it did,' said the old lady soothingly.

'I say it did,' replied the other. 'There was no thought about it; I had just—What's the matter?'

His wife made no reply. She was watching the mysterious movements of a man outside, who, peering in an undecided fashion at the house, appeared to be trying to make up his mind to enter. In mental connection with the two hundred pounds, she noticed that the stranger was well dressed, and wore a silk hat of glossy newness. Three times he paused at the gate, and then walked on again. The fourth time he stood with his hand upon it, and then with sudden resolution flung it open and walked up the path. Mrs White at the same moment placed her hands behind her, and hurriedly unfastening the strings of her apron, put that useful article of apparel beneath the cushion of her chair.

She brought the stranger, who seemed ill at ease, into the room. He gazed at her furtively and listened in a preoccupied fashion as the old lady apologized for the appearance of the room, and her husband's coat, a garment which he usually reserved for the garden. She then waited as patiently as her sex would permit, for him to broach his business, but he was at first strangely silent.

'I—was asked to call,' he said at last, and stooped and picked a piece of cotton from his trousers. 'I come from 'Maw and Meggins'.'

The old lady started. 'Is anything the matter?' she asked, breathlessly. 'Has anything happened to Herbert? What is it? What is it?'

Her husband interposed. 'There, there, mother,' he said, hastily. 'Sit down, and don't jump to conclusions. You've not brought bad news, I'm sure, sir, and he eyed the other wistfully

'I'm sorry—' began the visitor.

'Is he hurt?' demanded the mother, wildly.

The visitor bowed in assent. 'Badly hurt,' he said, quietly, 'but he is not in any pain.'

'Oh, thank God!' said the old woman, clasping her hands. 'Thank God for that! Thank—'

She broke off suddenly as the sinister meaning of the assurance dawned upon her and she saw the awful confirmation of her fears in the other's averted face. She caught her breath, and turning to her slower witted husband, laid her trembling old hand upon his. There was a long silence.

'He was caught in the machinery,' said the visitor at length in a low voice.

'Caught in the machinery,' repeated Mr White, in a dazed fashion, 'yes.'

He sat staring blankly out at the window, and taking his wife's hand between his own, pressed it as he had been wont to do in their old courting-days nearly forty years before.

'He was the only one left to us,' he said, turning gently to the visitor. 'It is hard.'

The other coughed, and rising, walked slowly to the window. 'The firm wished me to convey their sincere sympathy with you in your great loss,' he said, without looking round. 'I beg that you will understand I am only their servant and merely obeying orders.'

There was no reply, the old woman's face was white, her eyes staring, and her breath inaudible; on the husband's face was a look such as his friend the sergeant might have carried into his first action.

'I was to say that Maw and Meggins disclaim all responsibility,' continued the other. 'They admit no liability at all, but in consideration of your son's services, they wish to present you with a certain sum as compensation.'

Mr White dropped his wife's hand, and rising to his feet, gazed with a look of horror at his visitor. His dry lips shaped the words, 'How much?'

'Two hundred pounds,' was the answer.

Unconscious of his wife's shriek, the old man smiled faintly, put out his hands like a sightless man, and dropped, a senseless heap, to the floor.

III

In the huge news cemetery, some two miles distant, the old people buried their dead, and came back to a house steeped in shadow and silence. It was all over so quickly that at first they could hardly realize it, and remained in a state of expectation as though of something else to happen—something else which was to lighten this load, too heavy for old hearts to bear.

But the days passed, and expectation gave place to resignation—the hopeless resignation of the old, sometimes miscalled, apathy. Sometimes they hardly exchanged a word, for now they had nothing to talk about, and their days were long to weariness.

It was about a week after that the old man, waking suddenly in the night, stretched out his hand and found himself alone. The room was in darkness, and the sound of subdued weeping came from the window. He raised himself in bed and listened.

'Come back,' he said, tenderly. 'You will be cold.'

'It is colder for my son,' said the old woman, and wept afresh.

The sound of her sobs died away on his ears. The bed was warm, and his eyes heavy with sleep. He dozed fitfully, and then slept until a sudden wild cry from his wife awoke him with a start.

'*The paw!*' she cried wildly. 'The monkey's paw!'

He started up in alarm. 'Where? Where is it? What's the matter?' She came stumbling across the room towards him. 'I want it,' she said, quietly. 'You've not destroyed it?'

'It's in the parlour, on the bracket,' he replied, marvelling. 'Why?' She cried and laughed together, and bending over, kissed his cheek. 'I only just thought of it,' she said, hysterically. 'Why didn't I think of it before? Why didn't *you* think of it?'

'Think of what?' he questioned.

'The other two wishes,' she replied, rapidly. 'We've only had one.' 'Was not that enough?' he demanded, fiercely 'No,' she cried, triumphantly; 'we'll have one more. Go down and get it quickly, and wish our boy alive again.'

The man sat up in bed and flung the bed-clothes from his quaking limbs. 'Good God, you are mad!' he cried, aghast.

'Get it,' she panted; 'get it quickly, and wish—Oh, my boy, my boy!'

Her husband struck a match and lit the candle. 'Get back to bed,' he said, unsteadily. 'You don't know what you are saying.'

'We had the first wish granted,' said the old woman, feverishly; 'why not the second?'

'A coincidence,' stammered the old man.

'Go and get it and wish,' cried his wife, quivering with excitement. The old man turned and regarded her, and his voice shook. 'He has been dead ten days, and besides he—I would not tell you else, but—I could only recognize him by his clothing. If he was too terrible for you to see then, how now?'

'Bring him back,' cried the old woman, and dragged him toward the door. 'Do you think I fear the child I have nursed?'

He went down in the darkness, and felt his way to the parlour, and then to the mantelpiece. The talisman was in its place, and a horrible fear that the unspoken wish might bring his mutilated son before him ere he could escape from the room seized upon him, and he caught his breath as he found that he had lost the direction of the door. His brow cold with sweat, he felt his way round the table, and groped along the wall until he found himself in the small passage with the unwholesome thing in his hand.

Even his wife's face seemed changed as he entered the room. It was white and expectant, and to his fears seemed to have an unnatural look upon it. He was afraid of her.

'Wish!' she cried, in a strong voice.

'It is foolish and wicked,' he faltered.

'Wish!' repeated his wife.

He raised his hand. 'I wish my son is alive again.'

The talisman fell to the floor, and he regarded it fearfully. Then he sank trembling into a chair as the old woman, with burning eyes, walked to the window and raised the blind.

He sat until he was chilled with the cold, glancing occasionally at the figure of the old woman peering through the window. The candle-end, which had burned below the rim of the china candlestick, was throwing pulsating shadows on the ceiling and walls, until, with a flicker larger than the rest, it expired. The old man, with an unspeakable sense of relief at the failure of the talisman, crept back to his bed, and a minute or two afterward the old woman came silently and apathetically beside him.

Neither spoke, but lay silently listening to the ticking of the clock. A stair creaked, and a squeaky mouse scurried noisily through the wall. The darkness was oppressive, and after lying for some time screwing up his courage, he took the box of matches, and striking one, went downstairs for a candle.

At the foot of the stairs the match went out, and he paused to strike another; and at the same moment a knock, so quiet and stealthy as to be scarcely audible, sounded on the front door.

The matches fell from his hand and spilled in the passage. He stood motionless, his breath suspended until the knock was repeated. Then he turned and fled swiftly back to his room, and closed the door behind him. A third knock sounded through the house.

'*What's that*?' cried the old woman, starting up.

'A rat,' said the old man in shaking tones—'a rat. It passed me on the stairs.'

His wife sat up in bed listening. A loud knock resounded through the house.'

'It's Herbert!' she screamed. 'It's Herbert!'

She ran to the door, but her husband was before her, and catching her by the arm, held her tightly.

'What are you going to do?' he whispered hoarsely.

'It's my boy; it's Herbert!' she cried, struggling mechanically, 'I forgot it was two miles away. What are you holding me for? Let go. I must open the door.'

'For God's sake don't let it in,' cried the old man, trembling.

'You're afraid of your own son,' she cried, struggling. 'Let me go. I'm coming, Herbert; I'm coming.'

There was another knock, and another. The old woman with a sudden wrench broke free and ran from the room. Her husband followed to the landing, and called after her appealingly as she hurried downstairs. He heard the chain rattle back and the bottom bolt drawn slowly and stiffly from the socket. Then the old woman's voice, strained and panting.'

'The bolt,' she cried, loudly. 'Come down. I can't reach it.'

But her husband was on his hands and knees groping wildly on the floor in search of the paw. If he could only find it before the thing outside got in. A perfect fusillade of knocks reverberated through the house, and he heard the scraping of a chair as his wife put it down in the passage against the door. He heard the creaking of the bolt as it came slowly back, and at the same moment he found the monkey's paw, and frantically breathed his third and last wish.

The knocking ceased suddenly, although the echoes of it were still in the house. He heard the chair drawn back, and the door opened. A cold wind rushed up the staircase, and a long loud wail of disappointment and misery from his wife gave him courage to run down to her side, and then to the gate beyond. The street lamp flickering opposite shone on a quiet and deserted road.